# SHATTERED DREAMS

# SHATTERED DREAMS

Lynn Granger

CHIVERS
THORNDIKE

This Large Print book is published by BBC Audiobooks Ltd, Bath, England and by Thorndike Press®, Waterville, Maine, USA.

Published in 2005 in the U.K. by arrangement with the author.

Published in 2005 in the U.S. by arrangement with Dorian Literary Agency.

U.K. Hardcover   ISBN 1–4056–3369–7  (Chivers Large Print)
U.K. Softcover   ISBN 1–4056–3370–0  (Camden Large Print)
U.S. Softcover   ISBN 0–7862–7650–9  (British Favorites)

The text of this Large Print edition is unabridged.
Other aspects of the book may vary from the original edition.

Set in 16 pt. New Times Roman.

Printed in Great Britain on acid-free paper.

---

**British Library Cataloguing in Publication Data available**

---

**Library of Congress Cataloging-in-Publication Data**

Granger, Lynn.
    Shattered dreams / by Lynn Granger.
        p.    cm.
    "Thorndike Press large print British favorites."—T.p. verso.
    ISBN 0–7862–7650–9 (lg. print : sc : alk. paper)
    1. Teenagers—Services for—Fiction. 2. Scotland—Fiction.
3. Large type books. I. Title.
PR6107.R354S53 2005
823'.92—dc22                                              2005004930

---

# CHAPTER ONE

Roni had missed her turn again. She had hung back deliberately. All the old dread surfaced. The mere thought of sitting in a classroom again filled her with apprehension. They were called lecture rooms, here at the College of Further Education, but what difference would a name make? Her fellow students would laugh as they had done at school, or maybe snigger behind their hands. She shuddered. She half rose as panic gripped her.

'You've too much imagination, lass!' she could hear her grandmother's voice, brisk but always kindly. 'People are too busy with their own affairs to pay attention to yours, or should be if they've any sense.'

The large hall was beginning to empty. The young man next to her left his seat and headed for the table marked Basic Accounts—Stage 1. She clenched her fists, feeling them clammy with nerves. Why had she allowed herself to be persuaded? Of course, Mrs Boyd from the Enterprise Office had said she would need a set of accounts and a cash flow if she wanted financial assistance to comply with the hygiene regulations and the addition of a tea-room to her little market garden.

'Next please.'

The lecturer sounded weary and Roni's

heart sank, but she made her leaden limbs move to his table.

'You want to study accounts?' Joseph Cole asked with a frown.

'Oh, yes! Well, at least . . . I mean . . .'

'You mean your parents are pushing you into it?' Joseph suggested.

He pushed his fingers through his hair. He knew his personal anxiety was draining him of his usual enthusiasm and energy. He was used to reluctant students in his day-time classes. Inspiring them had always been a challenge he had enjoyed. He had expected the students who attended evening classes would supply their own motivation. He looked at the girl's bowed head.

'Sometimes parents can be wrong to . . .'

'It's not that. I haven't any parents.'

Her voice was low but without self-pity or resentment.

'I need to understand how to keep accounts, just simple ones. Please . . .' There was a note of desperation in her voice now, a plea in the troubled dark eyes staring earnestly at him across the table.

'If you have the desire to learn, that is more than half the battle. Tonight's enrolment is for Basic Accounts. I'm sure you will have no difficulty with that.'

'Oh, but you don't understand.'

'There's no need to be nervous,' Joseph said kindly. 'Here is the registration form.'

2

He turned it towards her and pushed it across the table.

'Just read the questions and fill in your name and address and the relevant details.'

Roni bit her lip and pulled the form closer, studying it intently, reading slowly. Painstakingly, she filled in her name and then her address. Her date of birth came next. So far, so good. Her brow creased anxiously as she read through a long paragraph of closely-typed information.

Joseph stole a glance at his wrist watch. He had promised Ruth he would get home as quickly as he could. He looked across at the girl's lowered head and wondered what was taking her so long. She was quite different to most of the other young women he had seen milling around the registration hall. Her face had a clean, newly-scrubbed look instead of the layers of make-up and mascara which seemed to be the rule from the age of eleven upwards.

His gaze moved back to the form. Her fingers were clenched tensely on the edge of the table and his eyes widened at the sight of her chipped and broken nails. Her hands were completely at variance with the baby-soft bloom on her rounded cheeks. Beneath the electric lights, her mane of dark hair gleamed. It was drawn back into a thick French pleat but the severe style suited her.

She had not filled in any of the other boxes.

He frowned, remembering his promise and the urgent need to hurry home to his wife and son. 'I'm afraid I must ask you to hurry now, Miss . . .'

He squinted at the form and read her name upside down.

'Miss Veronica Kennedy.'

'I—I—could you . . .'

Roni flushed with embarrassment.

'Would you fill it in for me? Please?'

Joseph opened his mouth to protest then decided it would probably be quicker to do as she asked. Besides, he found the plea in her eyes hard to resist. She reminded him of the spaniel they had bought for Simon's sixth birthday. What a happy day that had been. It seemed a whole lifetime ago instead of twenty years.

Swiftly he spun the sheet of paper towards him and scanned the questions, reading them aloud, filling in the boxes almost before Roni supplied the answers. He had almost finished. His head jerked up in surprise.

'What? No other qualifications? None at all?'

'N—no,' she stammered and felt the blood stain her cheeks, burning her up with shame. 'I tried. I really did, but . . .'

Suddenly the words came pouring out in a rush.

'I think . . . well . . . one of my teachers thought I might be dyslexic.'

Her face lost some of its tension as she remembered Mr Ling, the art teacher. He was the only one who had shown her patience and understanding and tried to help.

'I see. The school did not suggest any special help?'

'No, but I was ready to leave by then.'

'It is nearly four years since you left school. You must have been barely sixteen.'

Joseph looked up from the particulars in front of him.

'Yes. Granny, that is, my grandmother, was dying. I wanted to leave school. Grandfather needed me. I helped him in the gardens, you see, and I did the cooking, the things Granny had always done.'

Her eyes met Joseph's. His gaze was shrewd, but kindly.

'I wanted to leave school. I never liked it,' she added with a burst of honesty. 'In fact, I hated it.'

Joseph nodded.

'And your parents? Did they think you should leave school to look after your grandfather?'

'I told you, my parents are dead.'

'Both of them?'

Joseph was used to some pupils telling fabricated family histories. Roni nodded.

'I'm sorry, I didn't mean to pry,' he said quickly.

'That's all right. They were killed in an air

5

crash when I was nine months old so I never knew them.'

The hall was empty now, except for one other lecturer.

'I must go. Thank you. Good-night.'

Joseph watched her hurry to the other end of the hall, her long legs carrying her swiftly away from him. She moved with a natural grace, no exaggerated wiggle of the hips, no self-conscious shuffling. He frowned as he gathered up his papers and stuffed them into his briefcase. The girl puzzled him. She looked intelligent and she had nice manners. She had a lovely smile, faintly sad maybe, but there was nothing sullen or resentful in her demeanour.

'Will you join us for a drink at The Crown before you go home, Joe?'

The invitation from his fellow lecturer echoed across the empty hall.

'Thanks, Andy, but not tonight. I promised Ruth I wouldn't be late.'

'Simon still needing a lot of help, is he?'

There was sympathy and understanding in Andrew Woodward's tone. The two chatted amiably as they gathered up their belongings.

'I'll walk with you to your car.'

\*        \*        \*

When Roni had arrived at the college, the parking area had been crowded. In the fading light of the September evening she felt she had been lucky to find an empty space and she had edged her van into a gap between an estate car and the high brick wall which marked the boundary between the college carpark and a housing estate. Now the sky was a deep purple and the lights near the college entrance cast a yellow glow over the few cars still parked in the area reserved for staff. Her own vehicle seemed miles away, lost and forlorn in deep shadow by the wall. She zipped up her anorak against the autumn chill and hurried across the uneven ground.

As she inserted the key in the lock she thought she heard hoarse whispers, but her mind was on the best way to manoeuvre the van away from the wall.

'That's strange,' she muttered, eyeing its lopsided angle.

The van was almost touching the wall and she was sure she had not parked so closely. She was a good driver. She had to be with no money to spare for unnecessary repairs. She unlocked the van and reached for a torch. She groaned aloud when she saw the flat tyre.

Stifled laughter came from the other side of the wall.

'Hey, it isn't old Sparky! It's a woman!'

Roni heard the whisper and frowned. As she walked round to the other side of the van, the beam of her torch highlighted a tousled head and clinging hands before they disappeared behind the high wall.

'You're right, Jugs! It is a woman. We've picked the wrong one. That can't be Sparky's old banger.'

There was an audible gasp.

In dismay, Roni saw she had three flat tyres and she guessed the youths had done this deliberately. She felt like bursting into tears as the tensions of the day welled up inside her. This was the last straw, but crying wouldn't get her home. She had one spare tyre, but what use was that? She would have to telephone a garage and that would mean a hefty bill, but she had to get home and she needed the van tomorrow for her deliveries.

One of the few remaining cars revved up and drove away rapidly. Panic galvanised her into action. She would be left here alone, with only the vandals on the other side of the wall. She could still hear them whispering together.

Then she saw Mr Cole push open the swing doors and come out on to the steps with another man who was lighting a pipe. She hadn't known of Joseph Cole's existence until this evening but now he was the only familiar figure in this alien place. She sprinted up the deserted carpark, waving her torch to attract his attention, afraid that he might drive away before she reached him.

'Is there a public telephone I could use?' she gasped, reaching him as he slid into the seat of his own car.

Joseph looked up, recognising her as the

last student to register, but his mind was on his wife and son.

'It is just along the second corridor.'

'You'll have to be quick. The janitor will be locking up,' Andrew Woodward remarked laconically, glancing up from his pipe.

'Thank you. You don't know the number of the nearest garage, do you?' she asked hopefully.

'Garage?' The pipe paused in mid-air. 'Run out of petrol, have you?'

'No, I have not.'

Indignation and frustration banished Roni's desire to sit down and howl her head off.

'Someone has let the air out of three of my tyres. I think they may have damaged the valves. There are some boys hiding behind that wall. I heard them and I'm sure they did it deliberately.'

Try as she would to control it, her voice wobbled.

'Oh, dear.'

Joseph frowned and peered across the empty carpark.

'Well, you have left it in a rather deserted spot.'

'It wasn't deserted when I arrived. There was no other room at all.'

'No, no probably not. It's getting late now.'

Automatically he switched on the lights. Suddenly the full beam streamed across the park illuminating the head and shoulders of three figures before they disappeared behind the wall.

'That was Jon Goodsby!' Andrew exclaimed.

'You know them?'

'One of them for sure. He's a student. First year mechanics. They call him Jugs because he has such protruding ears.'

'I heard someone say Jugs. It doesn't mend my tyres though. I must phone . . .'

'I pass the garage on my way home,' Joseph said, stifling a sigh. 'I could drop you off.'

'Most of the garages will be closed by now,' Andrew Woodward said. 'It's too bad of those young hooligans. We could ask Jim Sparks if he would supervise some of his lads while they repair the damage tomorrow. He believes in giving them hands-on experience.'

'But I need my van to get home,' Roni protested. 'I need it tomorrow afternoon for deliveries.'

'Couldn't you catch a bus tonight and come back for your van tomorrow? It would be a lot cheaper than calling out the garage.'

'We don't have service buses at Bellingdale.'

'I live in that direction,' Joseph said resignedly, 'at Glendocken. I'll give you a lift, but I must call in at my home on the way and explain what has happened.'

Roni hesitated. Her van was vital for delivering the vegetable orders and she hated to be a nuisance to this weary-looking man, but it would take her for ever to battle her way through the telephone directory. The list of names and numbers confounded her.

'I don't have time to wait and I assure you it would be far better than roaming around the streets of Elldarwood on your own,' Joseph said wryly, misinterpreting Roni's anxious expression.

'It's not that,' she stammered. 'I really do need my van tomorrow. I grow vegetables and deliver them. I knew I should never have come tonight.' Her voice wavered.

'I'll have a word with Mr Sparky first thing tomorrow,' Andrew Woodward promised, holding the door open for her. 'We'll have the van back to you by lunch time.'

'Thank you. I'm sorry to be such a nuisance,' she added miserably.

'It's those young vandals who are a nuisance,' Andrew Woodward said grimly as he watched Joseph drive off with the girl.

Roni glanced at the profile of Mr Cole in the dim light from the dashboard. He looked tense and drawn.

'Soon be there now,' he said quietly, as the car eventually turned a sharp corner into the village of Glendocken. He drove into a small crescent of four detached houses and through wrought-iron gates. A light came on illuminating a curving flagged patio in front of a double garage with painted green doors.

'I'll just tell my wife what has happened

11

then I'll run you home.'

Joseph Cole was out of the car and striding to a side door before Roni could nod her head. Inside, he had barely finished explaining about the vandals before Ruth's concern was aroused, but the sight of his drawn face and tired eyes stilled her tongue.

'You look all in, Joe. There's plenty of food for one extra. Perhaps the girl could join us.'

'Are you sure? I'm certainly ready for . . .'

'If you're bringing some strange female in here I'm going to bed!'

Ruth and Joseph turned to face their son, sitting bolt upright in his wheel-chair.

'But, Simon, you haven't eaten either.'

'I've no intention of eating with a gaping stranger, just because Father sees fit to drag her in off the streets. Have you forgotten this is my home?'

Ruth gazed helplessly at her son, dismayed at the bitterness in his voice, the grim set to his thin face.

'We have never forgotten this is your home, Simon, or that we are your parents. You have never allowed us to forget for a moment, since the day we brought you home from hospital six weeks ago. The girl waiting out there doesn't even have parents.'

'Left her on the steps of an orphanage, did they?'

Joseph stared at his only son. Could this possibly be the same person who had worked

12

so hard to help the underprivileged lads in Glasgow'? He shook his head in despair.

'Oh, dear, he's been argumentative and bad-tempered all day,' Ruth said softly.

'Don't speak about me as though I'm not here,' Simon snapped, 'or as though I'm deaf, dumb and wrong in the head, as well as crippled.'

'The son we knew and loved is not here,' Joseph said quietly but there was a thread of steel in his voice which even Ruth had never heard before, and she glanced at him anxiously, as he went on, grimly. 'I shall invite Miss Kennedy in to share our meal. If you refuse to join us you can go to bed hungry.'

'I'll have mine in my room.'

'You eat with us, or not at all.'

'Stop treating me like a child!'

'Then stop acting like one.'

Joseph turned on his heel and strode to the door.

'Joe!'

Ruth laid a tentative hand on his arm.

'Perhaps it was not a good idea.'

Her eyes were pleading, her face strained and tired. Joseph raised a finger and drew it gently down her cheek, allowing it to rest briefly at her mouth. How drained she looked.

'Enough is enough,' he said firmly. 'I think you'll like Miss Kennedy. She's your kind of girl.'

Ruth blinked at his retreating back. What

13

was her kind of girl? A blue stocking studying accountancy? A girl bent on a successful career? She turned to face her son and found him with his head slumped in his hands. Her heart twisted at the sight of his utter dejection.

'Oh, Simon.'

She stroked the spiky hair which had once been so thick and wavy. Slowly it was beginning to cover the scars from the operation.

'Your father didn't mean to be harsh. You know how much we love you.'

'I don't see how you can love me. I hate myself, but I can't help it, Mother. I feel so useless! It would have been better if they'd left me to die.'

'Things will improve,' Ruth soothed softly.

Neither of them had heard the door open. Roni hesitated on the threshold and Joseph paused, too. To an outsider looking in, it was a cosy, lamplit room, with a loving mother comforting a son in pain or trouble. Just for a moment Roni felt a stab of envy. This was all so different from The Lodge which was her own home, so dark and empty now. Once it had been full of loving kindness, too.

She knew nothing of the tensions and storms which threatened the lives of the three people who were watching her with varying expressions of welcome, surprise, and was it resentment she saw in the grey eyes of the young man in the wheel-chair? But why should he resent her? He didn't even know her.

14

# CHAPTER TWO

Roni made an effort to respond to Mrs Cole's efforts at conversation but her admiration of the house was sincere so she was unprepared for Simon Cole's contemptuous snort.

'A lovely room! A delicious pie! Making sure you'll be invited back, are you?' he snapped.

Roni's cheeks flushed. Ruth caught her breath in dismay while Joseph stared at his son in angry disbelief.

'I am speaking the truth,' Roni answered quietly but her eyes flashed as they met and held the bitter grey gaze of the young man glaring at her across the table. 'You may think you are the only one with problems, but this was an awful day for me, too. Finding three flat tyres on my van seemed like the last straw. I am grateful for your father's offer of a lift, and your mother's invitation to share your meal.'

She waved a hand, Indicating the well-furnished room, the obvious quality of the thick carpet and toning velvet curtains which reached down to the floor, the wide, marble fire place where flames danced and flickered merrily, in addition to the warmth from the radiator at the back of her chair.

'No doubt you take all this comfort for

15

granted if you have had it all your life. To me it does look lovely. What is so wrong about saying so?'

Simon's only response was a cynical grunt but Roni was tired and tense and her patience was evaporating by the second. She had had a day full of doubts and dread.

'My grandparents could not provide the luxury of a home like yours, but they gave me all the love I needed and taught me good manners,' she went on angrily, 'enough manners never to angle for an invitation, especially when it is clear I am not welcome.'

She stood up, unaware that anger and indignation had added golden sparks to her dark brown eyes, or that the colour which flared on her cheeks added to her attraction.

'Oh, please! My dear,' Ruth Cole protested, 'I can only apologise for Simon's childish behaviour.'

Roni hesitated, glancing at the mocking face across the table. She badly wanted to escape but she was dependent on Mr Cole to drive her home.

'We have not had coffee yet. I really would like a cup, before we drive on to Bellingdale,' he said, looking tired.

'Of course,' Roni said apologetically and subsided on to her chair. 'It was thoughtless of me.'

'I'll bring it right now,' Ruth Cole said with relief. 'And, Simon, do remember it is not

Roni's fault that you've spent the past few months in a wheel-chair.'

'You have not been in a wheel-chair all your life then?' Roni asked.

'What difference does that make? I'm in one now and . . .'

'But not for ever, Simon,' Joseph Cole interrupted. 'The surgeon said there was a good chance you would learn to walk again if they could save your other leg and they do seem more hopeful now. Once your injuries have healed enough for you to be fitted with an artificial limb you will soon . . .'

'Make a fine Long John Silver to go lurching along the street for all the young hooligans to laugh at.'

'You spent most of your free time befriending and helping young hooligans, as you call them! Why should you expect them to mock you? Once you get out and about again you will . . .'

'I'll stay where I am.'

Simon gave a visible shudder and just for an instant, Roni glimpsed a terrible anguish in his eyes. The hollows and planes of his face seemed filled with despair and bewilderment. Then he turned sharply away towards the kitchen, willing his mother to hurry back with the coffee and end his evening's ordeal. Roni was equally relieved when Mrs Cole returned with the tray of coffee.

'Sorry, I'm afraid it is a bit crowded in here,'

she said ruefully as she squeezed past Roni's chair.

'You don't need to apologise to me,' she replied. 'When my grandmother had a stroke, we made a bed for her in the living-room and it is tiny compared with this. She liked to be with us so that she could see what was going on. Granny was so thankful just to be at home.'

'I'm sure she was, my dear.'

'Unlike me, I suppose!' Simon muttered.

'Don't look for criticism where none is meant,' his mother chided. 'I was merely . . .'

'Making polite conversation?'

'I think it is time I went home,' Roni said uncomfortably. 'That is unless I can help you wash the dishes?'

'Yes, dear, I would like that.' Ruth Cole smiled at her. 'Joseph can have five minutes with his paper. Anyway, it's not often I get an offer of help in the kitchen.'

'My fault again, of course!' Simon growled.

'Then perhaps you should do something about all your faults,' Roni flared in exasperation, and instantly regretted her outburst.

She looked at Ruth Cole in consternation.

Ruth Cole handed Roni the tray of dirty dishes and ushered her into the kitchen.

'Don't be upset. Spontaneous disapproval from someone of his own generation might well be good for Simon. Just for a moment there was a look of surprise on his face. At least it makes a change from boredom and bitterness.'

She handed Roni an empty tray.

'Will you bring the rest of the dishes through, please, dear?'

'So Miss cure-all, what do you suggest I do with my many faults? Get up and walk?' Simon challenged as soon as she re-entered the room.

'A glimpse of a smile would do for a start.'

'You've a sharp tongue! I don't envy my father having you for a student.' Roni escaped to the kitchen with her hastily-loaded tray.

'I really didn't mean to repay your hospitality by being rude to your son, Mrs Cole. I'm afraid I have really upset him. I'm not usually unsympathetic, or impatient.'

'Don't apologise, Roni. I am beginning to wonder if we have humoured him too much. You brought him alive. I hate to see him brooding in gloomy silence. To tell the truth, my dear, I've had as much as I can take from Simon recently, but I feel very guilty for admitting such a thing, especially to someone I scarcely know. You do seem very understanding for such a young person.'

'I'm afraid your son would not agree.'

'Maybe he wouldn't, but I think you were defending me, rather than criticising Simon. Joseph gives me all the support he can, of course, but he is so often out of the house and he is going to be even busier now that he is taking on evening classes. He hopes we may be able to pay for some kind of therapy to help Simon if he earns extra money.'

She rested her soapy hands on the edge of the washing-up bowl and turned her eyes to Roni.

'I must say, you seem very different to the usual run of students I hear about.'

'I expect that's because I was brought up by my grandparents. I'm more used to older people and I've always been content with my life, or at least I was, and I would still be, if things could have stayed the same.'

She went on polishing and re-polishing the plate she was drying.

Ruth was curious. Miss Veronica Kennedy was certainly different to any of the girls she had met when she was working at the office or when Simon had brought his friends to visit.

'You were enrolling for the accountancy class tonight? Do you intend to change your job when you finish the course?'

'Oh, no. I've too much work to do already, especially since grandfather died but the gardens don't make enough money to pay for hired help. I was thinking of trying a small tea-room in the summer to supplement my income.

'That sounds very business-like.'

'Mrs Boyd probably thinks I'm crazy. She's from the Local Enterprise Office, and she seems to believe it will solve all my problems if

I learn to do accounts. If only . . .'

She sighed and her brow puckered, and then she rubbed her fist in her eye in an oddly childlike gesture.

'And you, Roni, don't you think learning about accounts will help?' Ruth prompted feeling an unexpected interest in this refreshingly-innocent young woman.

'I know how much money I can make from the gardens, but I can't make projections and cash flows and present figures in the way the Enterprise people want them. If only I could try out the tea-room idea first to see if it would attract more customers. The trouble is the Environmental Health people have a lot of regulations which must be followed first, however small my tea-room.'

'What sort of regulations?'

'Oh, things like having two sinks and a separate wash-basin in the kitchen, another refrigerator, not to mention approved surfaces for the floor and walls and more storage areas.'

Roni positively groaned aloud this time. She had been over and over her situation many times. It sounded all right in theory when Mark Houston enthused about it, but she was the one who had to do the work and she couldn't be in two places at once. She loved the gardens and supplying the fresh vegetables to her regular customers.

'So you couldn't just do afternoon teas to try

21

it out?' Ruth asked.

'That's what I would like to have done, but it's impossible without approval. It was my friend who suggested I approach the Local Enterprise people. Tom and Janey got a grant when they took over a pub about four years ago. They have modernised it and renamed it the Silver Plume. Janey's brother, Mark Houston, is full of ideas. He loaned them some of the money so he is a partner but he works on the oil rigs and stays at the Silver Plume on his off-shore leave.'

'So you only want to learn about accounts to be able to present figures to the Local Enterprise?'

'Yes.'

'I'm sure you'll soon complete the course. I could ask Joseph to give you some guidance with your own accounts, if you like.'

'Oh, no, please don't do that. I don't think I shall be able to manage an accounts course at all, but everyone made me feel I ought to try. Anyway, I could never afford an accountant to present the figures for me.'

'Whatever makes you so sure you will not manage the course?'

'I was never any good at school,' Roni confessed in a low voice.

'Lots of people come to education when they are much older than you, these days, Roni. You are intelligent. What is to stop you?'

'You're very kind, but you see . . .'

She hesitated, wondering why she was confiding in this woman who was still a stranger. Then she looked up, her brown eyes pleading.

'I do mean to work hard but the trouble is there is always so much reading before I can even understand the questions. Time was always up before I understood the questions in the exam papers at school. I hated school! One of the teachers thought I was dyslexic and he said I should have had help before I left junior school, but most of the teachers just got impatient or angry. They didn't understand how hard I tried, and then I got angry, too. I wanted to learn, I really did.'

'You amaze me, Roni!'

Ruth Cole stared into the young, earnest face.

'You speak well and you strike me as having a very clear head. Perhaps you just need extra help.'

'Granny did her best. She thought I could read before I went to school. She used to read stories to me and I always knew what was coming next but it was just because I had heard them so often I could recognise the pictures. I must have been a great disappointment to her after my mother. She was a botanist, Dr Lindsay Anderson. Of course, she was Kennedy after she married my father but she kept her own name when she wrote her books. My grandparents were very

23

proud of her. Dad was an aircraft engineer and was actually on his way to inspect an aircraft when he was killed, flying over mountains in a storm. My mother had only decided to accompany him at the last minute. He had promised to take some leave and make a detour to help her search for a rare plant in the Andes.'

'How tragic! You poor child, to lose both of your parents.'

'I never knew them, and Granny and Grandpa made sure I never lacked for anything.'

Roni's smile was warm with remembered affection.

'They never let it show if they were ashamed of me.'

She broke off. Even now her face burned as one particular memory came rushing back. She had never told anyone, least of all Granny, about it, or the real reason she had begged so often to stay home from school. Miss Losnip, the teacher, had insisted she must read to the class. Roni felt she must know how much the dreaded reading aloud but she seemed to find satisfaction from making her do it. She had grown to hate and fear Miss Losnip's thin, hatchet face, the shiny beak nose and narrowed squinting eyes. She remembered stumbling her way through the dreaded sentences.

Her concentration on each separate word

had been so intense she had reached the end before she became aware of the tittering of her fellow pupils.

'Veronica Kennedy,' Miss Losnip snapped, 'in my book it says, "I saw the black cat up the tree", not, "I was a black cat up a tree". Now read the whole passage again.'

Roni still felt mortified. She would never forget the cruel teasing, the mimicking and taunting, which had lasted on and off until she and her classmates moved on to other schools. By then the damage to her fragile self-esteem had been done. She had stopped trying to keep up and she prayed for her school days to pass. Sometimes frustration had made her fly into a tantrum but Granny had always been calm and comforting.

Grandfather must have understood how she felt because he had not tried to change her mind when she begged to leave school. Perhaps he had realised how little time there was left for her beloved Granny, as the old lady had died within a few weeks of Roni's sixteenth birthday. After that it had seemed the most natural thing in the world that she should take over the running of the tiny house and help him with the gardens.

'I really don't know what I shall do if I can't make a living at the gardens,' she said now. 'The Lodge is the only home I've ever known and gardening is the only thing I know about. Oh, I'm so sorry, Mrs Cole. I shouldn't be bothering you with my problems. You have enough of your own.'

She smiled apologetically. Ruth Cole smiled back.


# CHAPTER THREE

Joseph Cole felt unutterably tired, but he knew it was more a tiredness of spirit as he drew the car to a halt at the entrance to a dark, tree-lined avenue flanked by two massive sandstone pillars. He guessed it was the drive to Bellingdale House.

As he turned the car, his lights picked up the shadowy outline of a quaint, stone lodge almost hidden by the curving boundary wall and the wrought iron railings on top of it. The Lodge had once guarded the southern entrance to the Bellingdale mansion. He felt uneasy at leaving a young woman alone in such a deserted and isolated place but there was little he could do.

He longed to get back to the warmth and comfort of his home, but it was no longer the haven of calm and peace at the end of a busy day. Simon's inability to come to terms with the changes which had been forced upon them all had caused a tension he and Ruth had never known before. They shared their son's misery but their anxiety for his future coupled with his dark moods exhausted them both.

Joseph wondered how much longer they could go on. Mentally Simon ought to be fit to resume his teaching career but he seemed unable to contemplate any kind of future. His world had turned upside down and he could see only bleakness in the life which stretched before him.

The doctors were unwilling, or unable to say how much independence he might regain. There had been mutterings about artificial limbs and invalid cars. So far, the police had not found the driver of the hit-and-run vehicle which had caused such havoc. It could take years of struggling before any compensation would be available to buy aids to a better life. The failure of the police investigations seemed to depress Simon more than anything else, as though something was preying on his mind, yet he could recall little of the accident himself.

He had been taking his leave of two of the older lads from the youth club and three or four more of his lads had been standing a few yards farther down the road. A vehicle had mounted the pavement, hitting him from behind, running over his legs. The injuries to his head had been caused by the fall and rendered him unconscious for several days. There had been no option but to amputate his left leg below the knee but they had done their best to save his right leg. Recently, the district nurse had been more optimistic as the wounds healed, but Simon seemed almost afraid to hope.

Joseph sighed. Teaching was the only thing Simon had ever wanted to do. He had devoted many of his evenings and Saturdays to the youth club, revelling in the challenges of the deprived area and the problems his lads faced. He had gained more satisfaction from the voluntary work there than he had from his paid employment. But whatever happened now, Simon would never be able to join in the sports and outdoor adventures which had earned the respect and confidence of the young people in one of the most notoriously violent parts of the city, but it was his son's mental scars which troubled Joseph. Neither he nor Ruth knew how to help him overcome the black and bitter depression and the doctors only prescribed time. But how much time? How much more could Ruth stand?

As they lay in bed later that night, Joseph was surprised to find how much his wife had enjoyed the visit of their unexpected guest. The girl's presence had clearly annoyed Simon though.

'At least he noticed her,' Ruth said. 'He roused himself from his silent stupor. That's the bit I find so depressing, so draining to my own spirits. It is totally unlike the son we knew. It's like having a stranger in the house and there's no reprieve.'

'He certainly noticed her all right,' Joseph

said. 'Simon always did thrive on a challenge. Perhaps that is what he is missing. We have been treating him with sympathy and velvet gloves all the time.'

Whatever Miss Veronica Kennedy's academic achievements, or lack of them, she had enough courage to hold her own in the face of Simon's hostility. Joseph found himself almost looking forward to his evening classes after all. At least one of his students had character and initiative. As he drifted into sleep, he wondered what his wife and Miss Kennedy had found to talk about for so long over the washing up.

*     *     *

Bellingdale South Lodge was the only home Roni could remember. She had always loved its tiny rooms with their mullioned windows and unexpected niches, but on this September night, with the autumn darkness intensified by the surrounding trees and the onset of a steady drizzle, the little lodge seemed forlorn and deserted, especially after the bright warmth and comfort of the Coles' home.

The darkness and isolation had never troubled Roni though. The thought of the dreaded classes held far more terror than the darkness ever would. Yet it was the bleakness in Simon Cole's grey eyes which stuck in her mind and made her shiver. He seemed to have no hope, no life, at least not one that he looked forward to living. He had made it abundantly clear that he resented her visit and she had no desire to repeat tonight's experience, except perhaps the kindness of Mr and Mrs Cole.

She shuddered as she remembered how easily she could have been stranded at the college, at the mercy of the thugs hiding behind the boundary wall. The thought focused her mind sharply on her dependence on the little van and her meagre budget for repairs. She prayed no further damage had been done. Perhaps she had been foolish to leave it in the deserted carpark overnight, yet what choice had she? She needed it tomorrow to deliver her vegetables to the greengrocer out at Pendonbrae and farther up the glen to Waylan. She hoped Mr Woodward would keep his promise and get it back to her in time.

Surprisingly, it was not her own problems which filled her mind as she fell asleep. It was the recollection of the graduation photograph of a happy, laughing young man in the home of Joseph and Ruth Cole. She wondered if the warmth of laughter would ever chase away the wintry ice in Simon Cole's eyes, or curve the grim set of his mouth into that wry, optimistic grin again.

The following morning, Roni worked her way steadily along the raspberry canes, cutting out the old ones and tying in the young canes which would bear next year's fruit. It was a job she usually enjoyed but her mind was constantly flitting back to her van. Just after midday, she made her way dispiritedly back to the lodge.

In the small kitchen she pushed a pan of soup on to the oil-fuelled stove and made herself a substantial cheese and chutney sandwich. After a morning's work in the open air even anxiety could not spoil her appetite.

Thoughts of the trays of fresh vegetables waiting to be delivered had just brought her mind back to her van when the silence was shattered by the screech of a motorbike. She recognised the head emerging from the big blue crash helmet at once and her heart beat faster. Last night it had been dark but she was sure it was the fellow called Jugs. Her blood chilled. How had he found her? Had he brought a troop of other motorcyclists? What did he want?

Then, to her intense relief, she saw the red van coming through between the stone pillars which flanked the entrance to the drive. She ran outside, her face alight with relief and gratitude. Andrew Woodward's brows rose at the attractive picture she made as her long, jean-clad legs leaped down the shallow flight of stone steps and came to a halt beside the van.

'Anyone would think this old van of yours was a long-lost friend,' he said with a grin. 'I

31

wish my wife greeted me half as rapturously.'

'Right now it's the most precious thing in the world to me,' Roni replied laughingly, tossing back the long thick pleat of hair which had bounced over her shoulder.

'Really? A pretty girl like you going into ecstasies over a bundle of old metal?'

'I need it to make my deliveries this afternoon,' Roni explained. 'I can't afford to let my customers down or I shall have nothing to live on.'

'You hear that, young Goodsby? You and your pals could have caused this young lady to lose good business with your pranks.'

'Aye, we're sorry, miss. We thought it was Mr Sparks' car. He's the engineering lecturer, see. He often brings his old wrecks in and makes us do 'em up for him, so . . .'

'He teaches you how to carry out practical maintenance and repairs,' Andrew Woodward corrected firmly.

'Mm, so you thought my poor little van was an old wreck, too, did you?' Roni grinned wryly and Andrew Woodward was again amazed at the transformation a smile could make.

'Do you really earn money delivering vegetables, miss?'

'Amongst other things,' Roni said. 'But that's the easy bit. I have to grow them first.'

'Grow them! You grow cabbages and carrots and things? Here?'

32

'Why, yes, in the gardens. They're just along that path there, through the trees.'

'Nobody round us has a garden. Can I see?' he said.

'Miss Kennedy has other things to do with her time,' Andrew Woodward intervened, 'and so have we. I shall have a room full of young rebels waiting for me at two o'clock and you'll be in trouble if you miss any more classes.'

The boy looked disappointed. Then his grubby face brightened.

'Can I come back another day, miss, to see your garden, I mean?'

'Now, Goodsby, Miss Kennedy doesn't want any more trouble from you and your gang,' Andrew Woodward warned grimly, and Roni saw a look of consternation on his pleasant face. 'I wouldn't have brought you if I'd thought you would . . .'

'But, sir, I'm not meaning any trouble. I had a window-box once. I planted it with seeds. Dad made it for me before he went off and left us. Bragger Dobson was jealous and broke it up. He didn't even wait for the seeds to grow.'

It was Roni's turn to stare now. The boy's anger and disappointment obviously still lurked in the shadows of his eyes, the droop of his mouth.

'You can come to look round if you're really interested,' she said, forgetting that he had helped to vandalise her van.

'And how are you going to get out here?'

Andrew Woodward asked, frowning his displeasure at the youth. 'And, no, before you even ask, you cannot borrow my motorbike. Today was a one-off, and you can ride pillion on the way back. I'd like to arrive in one piece. I'll just get my helmet out of the van and we'll leave you to get on, Miss Kennedy. You turn the bike around and wait for me at the gates, Goodsby.'

'I haven't thanked you,' Roni said.

'Nothing to thank us for.'

He smiled and lowered his voice.

'Jugs is not a bad lad really, but he's in with a bad crowd just now. He and his young sister haven't had much of a chance since their father left.'

'It makes me feel fortunate to have all this.'

Roni sketched a hand at the trees and flowers.

'Even if it is impossible to get through all the work I ought to do.'

'Surely you don't run this place on your own?'

Andrew felt he sounded as incredulous as young Goodsby.

'It was Grandfather's until he died three months ago. We worked the gardens between us.'

'And now it's yours?'

'Yes.'

'It must be worth a tidy sum!' Andrew said. 'You could sell a few building plots and live off

the income instead of slaving away here. No?'
he asked seeing Roni shaking her head
emphatically.

'Definitely not. Anyway, I don't think of
myself as slaving. Most of the time I love the
work with the plants and soil, growing things,
you know. In any case, Sir Callum Mackenzie,
the previous owner, made a provision that the
land must never be used for building purposes.
I can live here for ever, so could my children if
I had any, but we could never sell it.'

'But that's archaic! It can't be possible to
make such a condition, can it?'

'I think it must be. Sir Callum's lawyers
drew up the deeds. Anyway, he was very
generous and it is what he wanted. I think he
was trying to protect a small part of the
countryside he had grown to love, as well as
making sure my grandparents and I had a roof
over our heads for as long as we need one. The
rest of the grounds and the big house belong
to his great nephew now. He has put it up for
sale without even seeing it. Of course he does
live in Australia and I think he has thousands
of acres of land there.'

'I see. I suppose the old man guessed that
would happen. At least he made sure you had
some security.'

'Yes. It would have broken grandfather's
heart if he'd had to move. His own
grandfather, and his great grandfather, were
born at Bellingdale South Lodge. I am the last

of the family to work in the gardens. I only hope I can manage to carry on now that we're no longer part of the estate.'

'Is that why you're studying accounts with Joseph, so that you can keep an eye on your profits, eh? Well, I'm sure you'll be a success.'

'Sir! Mr Woodward, sir, are you coming?' Jugs called.

'Yes,' Andrew replied and grinned at Roni. 'Impatient young rascal. I hope the van goes well.'

*     *     *

Three weeks later, Joseph Cole voiced his ongoing doubts to his wife.

'Roni seemed such an intelligent young person,' Ruth protested.

'I think she is, basically.'

Joseph frowned. He hated to feel he was failing any of his students, or that he was not getting the best out of them.

'The strange thing is she can come up with the answers as quickly as any of the others when I ask questions in class. She has plenty of commonsense and ideas, but set her to do a written exercise, and she has scarcely done the first question by the time the class is over.'

'Sounds to me as though she can't understand the exercises.'

Joseph and Ruth spun round to stare at their son. He rarely spoke except in

36

monosyllables, and only then to answer a direct question or to make a resentful request for assistance. He had never joined in their conversations since the accident.

'Well, it is possible, for goodness' sake!' he snapped.

'Yes, it is,' his father agreed.

Was it possible Simon's interest in teaching was returning after all? He had always found the most difficult students a challenge.

'But the exercises are so simple at the beginning,' Joseph explained. 'Far simpler than the accounts Miss Kennedy must be doing for her market garden business, keeping track of income and expenses.'

'She runs a business?'

Simon blinked. He remembered the girl clearly, her fresh complexion, the healthy glow, long legs and slender figure, but surely she was too young to be a hard-headed business woman. She had seemed . . . well . . . gentle . . . no! That was not the word. She had been anything but gentle with him. In fact she had been pretty sharp.

'She has a small market garden,' his mother said. 'She helped her grandfather and I believe he kept the accounts before he died. Roni has only been on her own three months. I hope she doesn't get herself into difficulties with debts and things. She seemed such a nice girl.'

'That's her affair,' Simon muttered gruffly.

'Perhaps it is,' his mother retorted sharply,

'but she is absolutely alone in the world. She has no relatives at all so far as she knows, certainly no-one close. I wonder if I could help her.'

'But accountancy was never your field, dear,' Joseph remarked.

Later, in the privacy of their bedroom, he returned to the subject of Roni.

'I am concerned about that girl, you know, Ruth. Of all the students in the class she has the most incentive to complete the class but I have a feeling she is on the point of giving up. I can't help wondering if she really is dyslexic, as one of her teachers once suggested. I thought she was just making excuses for not having any other qualifications the night she enrolled, but she really does try.'

'Are you thinking of taking on extra coaching?'

'Not exactly, but did you notice how Simon joined in the conversation when I was telling you about Roni's difficulties?'

'Yes, but it's time he stopped brooding and realised other people have problems, too. We used to have such good discussions. You know I love him dearly but it gets me down seeing him staring glumly into space.'

'I know and it made me wonder if he and Miss Kennedy might help each other, without either of them being aware of it. If I suggested helping her, Simon might begin to take an interest.'

'I don't know.' Ruth hesitated. 'I really like Veronica Kennedy. I would hate to see her getting hurt and Simon can be so abrupt these days, almost as though he wants to hurt people.'

'Her problems could perhaps stimulate Simon's interest and some young company would be good for him. What do you think, Ruth?'

'I had thought of driving out to Bellingdale to buy some home-grown vegetables on Saturday. I could invite Roni for another meal. You can see what you think then.'

The September morning next day was bright and crisp and Ruth Cole felt her spirits rise as she drove along the quiet road towards Bellingdale Gardens. She found Bellingdale Lodge and its gardens without difficulty but she was surprised to hear the sound of laughter as she climbed out of the car. She lifted her head with pleasure at the scent of woodsmoke and behind the trees a lazy curl drifted into the air.

Ruth felt like a prisoner who had been granted unexpected freedom! She drank in the sounds and scents and sights, while the peace of the countryside washed over her like a healing balm. She took several deep breaths and felt herself relax. Then she followed the sounds until she came to a small bonfire on a bare patch of ground.

There she saw Roni smiling as she

supervised a scrawny lad who was feeding the flames with bundles of garden debris. He turned to Roni with a look which Ruth could only describe later to her husband as one of gratitude and wonder. Roni glanced up and saw Ruth standing beneath the trees. She came hurrying over, her brown eyes warm and welcoming.

'I can't believe this!' she exclaimed. 'Two unexpected visitors in one day.'

"The young man, he is not . . .' Ruth began.

'He is studying car mechanics at the college,' Roni broke in and lowered her voice. 'He is one of the boys who vandalised my van but Mr Woodward brought him out here to deliver it after it was repaired. His proper name is John Goodsby but he seems to be more familiar with Jugs.'

'I see,' Ruth said doubtfully. 'You don't mind him coming here then?'

'I couldn't,' Roni said. 'This is the second Saturday he has been. He thumbed a lift, but both times he has walked at least three miles from the road junction just to get here. He's desperately eager to help but he doesn't know the first thing about gardening. How could he, without so much as a tub at home to grow anything?'

'Well, you're very forgiving, my dear. I just hope he doesn't bring the rest of his gang of thugs out here to bother you.'

'Yes, I must say that does trouble me a bit,

but so far he has behaved really well and he's quite strong in spite of his skinny looks. I can certainly use all the help I can get. There's so much to do and I can't afford hired help. Jugs knows that but he says he just wants to come. Last week I gave him some potato soup and home-made scones. I don't think he has ever eaten anything that didn't come straight from a packet or a tin. He looked so wary! Then after a few spoons he wolfed it down. He had three bowls of soup and demolished most of the scones. He said it was better than being paid because his mother would just spend it at the bingo or at the pub.'

'Poor lad,' Ruth Cole sympathised. 'Well, so long as he doesn't get up to any more mischief it may be of benefit to both of you.'

'Oh, I expect he'll soon get bored and stop coming. Now, can I get you a cup of coffee?'

'Oh, no, thank you, dear. I haven't come to hinder you. I wanted to buy some carrots and onions, and I saw you had a tray of lovely cauliflowers, and some broccoli, too, as I came past your house.'

'They are for the Greenlands Hotel but I have plenty more if you'll come along this path.'

Ruth found it easy to suggest another visit to Glendocken but she was disappointed when Roni did not seize the opportunity as she had hoped.

# CHAPTER FOUR

Ruth made several visits to the lodge after that first one to buy fresh vegetables and eventually Roni was persuaded to visit Glendocken for a meal. She gave Joseph Cole a diffident smile as she accepted a glass of white wine and soda on her arrival. Tonight he was her host but he was also the lecturer of the accounts class and she had already skipped two sessions. With a sinking heart she knew she would skip the rest of them, too. She simply could not keep up with the rest of the group.

At first she had wondered if Ruth Cole's invitation to dinner was an excuse to persuade her to keep on going, but in fairness she had to admit the first invitation had come before she had skipped any of the classes. Anyway, she felt there was a growing rapport between them which bridged the generation gap and she appreciated the older woman's friendship. Even better, she sensed the feeling was mutual. Ruth Cole seemed to enjoy, even need, the short drives to Bellingdale and the peace of the gardens.

Twice they had wandered companionably through the grounds of the empty mansion house and along the short stretch of the river which bordered her own gardens.

'At least you are punctual,' Simon remarked

as he came into the room. His tone was amiable and Roni turned her attention to him.

'I try to be, especially when your mother is kind enough to invite me for a meal.'

She felt wary in his presence and she wasn't looking forward to another evening of Simon Cole's dark moods, and yet she felt challenged in some way, as though to refuse to visit was giving in, conceding victory, but what victory? She had had no fight with him. The fight, if there was one, was with himself, or with the world in general. She knew his moods affected everyone around him, most of all his mother.

'In my experience, women are rarely punctual, whatever the occasion.'

Simon knew the statement was without foundation. He just felt a need to ruffle the calm innocence of the young woman who reminded him painfully of a fresh, spring day. He could just imagine her with the wind in her hair, running through woods, scattering leaves hither and thither.

'You must have met a very poor selection of women,' Roni challenged, unwilling to let him get away with such a provocative statement. 'I can't imagine your mother making a habit of being late for appointments.'

'Ah, but Mother is different. There's few women like her.'

'I wish you'd tell her that sometime, son!' Joseph Cole said.

'I expect she knows. You must have told her

often enough.'

Simon's tone was even, but for a fleeting instant Roni glimpsed a look of such pain and desolation in his grey eyes that she felt a pang of pity, something she had never expected to feel for the embittered, selfish person she had judged him to be at their first meeting. She wondered if Joseph Cole had noticed, too, for his tone was gentle.

'That's not the same as you telling her. It breaks her heart to see you unhappy and not be able to make you better as she did when you were a child.'

Simon grimaced but he made no response. Nevertheless Roni felt he was making an effort to be pleasant when his mother brought in the meal. Ruth was delighted when he asked for a second helping.

'Maybe your appetite is returning at last,' she said with satisfaction, but Simon gave a mocking shrug when Roni met his glance.

'Father tells me you run a market garden,' he remarked, watching her collect the dishes while Ruth put the finishing touches to the scrumptious chocolate soufflé she had made for dessert.

'Well, I'm not sure you'd call it a market garden exactly,' Roni demurred. 'It's very small.'

'But you make a living?'

'I don't know yet. I haven't been on my own long. I'd like to expand.'

She pursed her lips and shrugged, unwilling to bore him with her problems.

'Tell me about it. At least market gardening is something new to talk about.'

The bitterness was back, but Roni felt it was not aimed directly at her this time.

'I thought of opening a small tea-room to attract more customers in the summer, but there are so many regulations.'

'So?'

'I explained it all to your mother.'

'That's not the same as telling me.'

'Are you really interested or just being polite?' Roni said awkwardly.

Simon's dark brows rose in surprise.

'A bit of both, I suppose, but at least I'm making an effort. So tell me.'

Roni repeated her plans for a tea-room and her application to the enterprise people.

'But they want all sorts of facts and figures.'

She glanced at Joseph Cole with an apologetic smile.

'Your father knows that's the reason I needed to learn to keep proper accounts.'

'Surely an accountant could present the figures for you?'

'Oh, yes, if I had the money to pay one, and if I had the sort of figures he would need in the first place. I told you, it really is a very small business. Gran and Grandpa used to be employed up at Bellingdale House until Sir Callum Mackenzie died. After that, Grandpa began to build up the market garden for himself. We had enough for our needs and we were very happy.'

Simon looked at her intently, bringing the colour to her cheeks.

'Yes,' he said slowly. 'Yes, I believe you really mean that.'

'Why shouldn't I mean it?' Roni's colour deepened.

'Because it takes so much to please most people. Everyone seems to want the things they have little hope of having, like me wanting two good legs.'

To Roni's amazement, he gave a rueful smile. It was an attractive smile, too, and for some reason she could not define, she felt extraordinarily pleased.

'I suppose you're right,' she replied thoughtfully.

'What, even in your case? What is the one most important thing you would like to have if someone could grant you a wish,' he asked curiously.

Behind his paper, Joseph Cole listened to his son's conversation with baited breath. He had almost forgotten what it was like to hear Simon's musing tones, the deep, slow voice. He had grown to expect the curt, monosyllabic answers. Then he heard Roni's reply.

'There is only one thing I would wish for, but no-one can grant it, any more than they can restore your own leg to you. But at least in your case they can give you a substitute leg.'

'A substitute!' Simon snorted angrily. 'Well, come on, tell me what it is you want,' he demanded impatiently, but his changed tone had destroyed Roni's urge to confide and she shook her head.

Simon glared. He was not pleased by her refusal. He wanted to know what she craved. It seemed important that he should know.

'You're cheating!' he accused angrily.

'And you sound like a small boy who has just lost a game of snakes and ladders.'

'All right, school ma'am!'

'That's one thing I could never be!'

'Why not? Are school teachers so abhorrent?'

'Yes. No . . . I mean it's just that I never liked mine and I could never be one anyway.'

'You would probably be a very good one if you are so aware of the effects a bad one can have on a sensitive child.'

'What's this about a sensitive child?' his mother asked returning with the soufflé.

'Roni doesn't like school teachers,' Simon explained.

'You don't?' Ruth said, looking dismayed. 'School teachers in general or Joseph and Simon in particular?'

'Oh!'

Roni clapped her hand to her mouth and blushed.

'I wasn't being personal! I don't think of

47

Mr Cole as a teacher.'

'That bad, am I, m'dear?'

'Oh, no, but surely a lecturer is different.'

'A bit perhaps, but my aim is still to get my subject across to students like yourself.'

'You'd have a hard task if they were all like me,' she said glumly.

'But not an impossible task.'

Suddenly the opening was there for him.

'If you're finding things a bit difficult to follow you could always bring some of your own accounts here. They would probably make far more sense than exercises. I could show you how to set them out properly and you'll be drawing up a balance sheet in no time.'

'Would you really show me what to do with Grandfather's figures?' Roni asked, her face as eager as a child's, her brown eyes alight.

Joseph glanced briefly at his wife.

'Yes, of course.'

He ignored his son's frown.

'There's not much opportunity for personal attention during the classes. Anyway, the other students don't have their own accounts, that's why we have to set all sorts of exercises. Could you come over here once a week?'

'Oh yes, if . . .'

She looked questioningly at Ruth.

'I think it's a splendid idea.'

Roni could not doubt her sincerity. Indeed she looked as satisfied as if she had thought of the idea herself.

'I don't know how I would repay you though,' she added doubtfully.

'You have already paid your enrolment fee to the college and if I can help you achieve your goal that will be reward enough,' Joseph said kindly.

'How about bringing us some more of those fresh vegetables?' Simon said.

'Simon!' Ruth exclaimed.

'I would be glad to do that, if you would accept them,' Roni assured her. 'I would feel much better if I was doing something in return.'

'Yes.' Simon nodded. 'Everyone needs to give something in return.'

His voice was bleak and Ruth's heart ached for him. She knew how much he resented his constant need of help. Even as a small boy he had been incredibly independent. He had found great satisfaction from his voluntary work, helping the more deprived boys at the club in Glasgow, but he had encouraged them to help themselves, and each other.

As the following weeks passed, Simon found himself taking an interest in Roni's progress in spite of his determination to remain aloof. He was astonished at her knowledge of gardening and plants, the seeds, fertilisers and treatments. Yet her spelling and reading ability were halting and uncertain. She lacked confidence and frequently made mistakes when writing down figures. Usually he was careful not to let her see his dismay at the glaring errors and he never allowed himself the smallest smile at her peculiar spellings.

Roni found herself enjoying sifting through the dog-eared pages of her grandfather's notebooks, entering the figures into columns as Joseph had suggested, but it was Simon who discussed the various aspects of her small business and helped her categorise the items of income and expenditure. He seemed genuinely interested and it was he who finally prepared the columns with their written headings. She wondered if he had guessed how much she dreaded entering them herself.

'It's really quite interesting to see which crops prove most profitable,' he mused one evening. 'It is not always the ones you expect. We did quite well with the brassica seedlings.'

She sighed.

'I ought to keep them going because we already have a number of regular customers in the spring. It takes a lot of time and labour pricking them all out though and it was one of the tasks Grandfather enjoyed right to the end.'

'He could manage that?' Simon asked in surprise.

'Oh, yes. He used to sit in his chair in front of the bench and work away to his heart's content. I kept him supplied with trays of seedlings so that he didn't have to get up unless he wanted to.'

'Didn't he get bored?'

'Never. Sometimes we talked, made plans for the garden for another year. Sometimes we listened to the radio. We both enjoyed listening to a good play while we worked with the seedlings, or music. Anyway, I can see already that it is much better to itemise some of the things instead of lumping them all together. I'm even beginning to understand why Mrs Boyd was so insistent I should learn to do it, but I can't imagine me ever presenting the figures well enough to prove I'm worthy of the financial assistance which is supposed to be available to small businesses.'

'Of course you will, once you get the hang of it. I had only done accounts for the boys' club before.'

Roni saw a shadow pass over Simon's face, but then she was delighted to hear him go on.

'But even I am finding this gardening business intriguing. I had no idea there were so many things to consider.'

He grinned unexpectedly at her enthusiastic face. She was so natural and at ease, almost childish in her gratitude, but there was nothing childish about her beauty, and the flowery scent of her skin and hair when she was working close beside him. The amazing thing to Simon was that she appeared to be totally unaware of her feminine attractions.

After a session of crouching over the books,

she would stand up and stretch her arms above her head as naturally and as gracefully as a young gazelle. Eyeing her long legs in the close-fitting blue jeans, seeing the narrow waist when jeans and jumper parted, Simon felt alive in a way he had never expected to feel again. He was a man, a young man with a man's desires, but he was also a cripple now. He must never forget that. He could not prevent the dark clouds which descended upon him at such times.

They came at the most unexpected moments, making him abrupt and taciturn. Roni invariably concluded he was bored with her company and gathered up her books, and at such times, not even Ruth Cole's coaxing could persuade her to stay.

Inwardly, Simon would curse himself for his moods, but outwardly he glowered silently, knowing that his parents could only shake their greying heads in bewilderment.

The consultant at the local hospital had decided it might be possible to manage without another operation and he realised Simon was in need of stimulation, both mental and physical. He arranged an appointment with the chief consultant at the Glasgow hospital where Simon had spent so many miserable weeks after the accident. He had no desire to return and he tried every excuse, but to no avail.

'We have volunteers who drive patients up

for appointments, so there will be no problem over transport,' the doctor assured him, brushing aside his protests. 'It's high time we were getting some of those muscles back into shape, but I need your surgeon's opinion before I proceed with my own ideas for getting you on your feet again.'

Simon could not suppress a snort of derision, although he appreciated the doctor was doing his best.

'You'll be surprised what can be achieved, given co-operation between a patient and his medical team. Have the police charged the driver who caused all this, by the way?'

Simon shook his head.

'They've nothing to follow up, so they say. I couldn't identify anyone.'

Privately, he was convinced some of the lads from the club must have seen what happened. Had they recognised the vehicle? Were they shielding one of their gang rather than help him? He thought he had earned their respect and their loyalty and their silence depressed him as much as the loss of his limb. Whenever he contemplated the accident, his spirits plummeted and the dark depression descended upon him. He was powerless to fight it. He felt deserted, let down.

His lads had failed him when he really needed their help, but he must have failed, too. Surely if he had truly earned their respect they would have supported him at such a time.

He knew how much they all hated any involvement with the law; but they could have visited him in hospital, just once, to tell him whatever they had seen. He knew they were incredibly loyal to their own kind. Obviously they had not regarded him as one of them.

'Someone will be charged, surely?' the doctor interrupted his thoughts, frowning. 'You'll be needing money, compensation and a car to help you get around in due course. You still have a life to live.'

'Don't remind me!'

'I know money can't give you back two healthy limbs, or compensate for all the pain you've suffered, but it can help to make life more bearable, get you some help in obtaining the latest aids so that you can regain a measure of independence. Consider your parents, too, Simon. They are making sacrifices to care for you, I'm sure. Why not enquire about legal aid, anything to help you snap out of this lethargy!'

Simon grimaced but he made no reply and the doctor shook his head, understanding the despondency, yet exasperated that he could not penetrate the apathy and arouse the inner strength and determination he was certain this young man possessed.

Simon was relieved to see that the volunteer chauffeur on the day of the Glasgow trip was a stern-faced man and not a fussy, middle-aged woman, intent on doing good deeds. He could not have coped with that for the hundred-mile round trip to Glasgow and back. The man was strong, too. He helped him into the car with the minimum of fuss. Then he stowed in the folding wheel-chair. Simon summoned a ghost of a smile and a sketchy wave to his mother as she hovered uncertainly to wave him off.

It wasn't long before his driver's stern expression gave way to a wry smile and Simon learned that Dick Ross was a retired police sergeant, and a widower. He enjoyed a captive audience and did not seem to mind Simon's preoccupation and terse responses as he regaled him with stories of his experiences in police forces in various parts of Scotland. He was a competent driver and really quite amusing in a gruff, sardonic manner. Simon gradually relaxed and found himself smiling, almost in spite of himself, as his new companion recounted some of the more lighthearted tasks in a policeman's daily round.

It was only when the car drew up outside a modern, glass-fronted hospital extension and he saw the hospital signs that Simon's morose mood returned and with it the sick despair. To make matters worse, he was suddenly reminded that it would soon be Christmas by two young nurses applying colourful stencils of a huge Santa, complete with sleigh and prancing reindeer, to the large windows.

'Oh, no,' he said, 'I don't know why I ever

agreed to come back here.'

Dick Ross looked at his white face with concern but he had dealt with all kinds of situations in his working life. He hid his compassion and his tone was brisk.

'Come on, young man, let's have you inside. These folks are too busy for the likes o' you and me to keep them waiting.'

It seemed an interminably long day to Simon, with X-rays and examinations, discussions and asides, consultations and instructions, but eventually he was left alone in a small room with a young woman dressed in a neatly-fitted white tunic and smart navy trousers.

'I'm a physiotherapist, Mr Cole, Sue Vine's the name.'

She extended a hand and shook Simon's firmly.

'Mr Lewisham, the surgeon who patched you up after your accident, and Dr Jennings at your local hospital, both think it's high time you were having more exercises now they are sure we are going to keep your other leg. It has healed far better than anyone expected. There are various treatments we would like to try,' she hurried on, refusing to give him any opportunity to argue. 'You really need daily therapy. Unfortunately, we can't offer you that here. Presumably you can get to your local hospital.'

'No! No, I can't do that!'

Simon had a mental picture of his mother struggling to get him out of the wheel-chair and into the car every day. Sue Vine frowned.

'You have no wife to assist?'

'No, I'm not married, nor ever likely to be now,' he muttered in an undertone, but the physiotherapist had heard him.

'Why not? Your pelvis wasn't injured, was it? It was only the lower part of your legs.'

'Only!'

Simon wanted to shake her until her bones rattled.

'Only your legs,' he jeered. 'And who on earth would want to marry a man without legs?'

'Oh, you'd be surprised,' Sue Vine said, unperturbed by his anger. 'After all, you're not such a bad looking young fellow.'

Simon glowered. Was she mocking him?

'That is when you're not frowning, fit to make it snow,' she added. 'Can you afford to have treatment at home?' she asked hopefully. 'I have a friend who lives down your way. We trained together but she's married now.'

'Private you mean? No chance,' Simon replied flatly.

'Mm, that's a pity. It would have suited Claudia to have a few private patients. She has three-year-old twins and a toddler so she could use the extra money, but she needs to fit in a few hours when her husband is at home to take care of the children. And she's good. I

57

reckon she has healing in her finger tips.'

Simon frowned reflectively.

'Maybe I should take Dr Jennings' advice and get a solicitor to try for compensation.'

'You haven't done that yet?' Sue Vine said in surprise.

'Money was the last thing on my mind but if it would procure anything to improve this rotten mess . . .' Simon muttered, glaring down at his offending limbs.

Before Sue Vine could answer there was a tap on the door.

'Enter,' she called. 'Aah, you must be Mr Cole's driver.'

She smiled when Dick Ross appeared in the room.

'That's me. The girl in reception thought he would be waiting for me to take him home.'

'Yes, we're just about ready. We were discussing arrangements for getting him to physiotherapy at his local hospital. You should get on to the police,' she said, turning back to Simon. 'Surely they can speed up proceedings? Some of them need a rocket, if you ask me.'

Simon's eyes met the twinkling eyes of Dick Ross.

'Oh, so that's what you think of the boys in blue, eh?' Dick chuckled. 'Just as well I'm retired then.'

'You were a policeman?'

Sue's cheeks flushed but she shrugged philosophically.

'Well, you would have thought they must have got somebody for a hit-and-run accident like this. He really ought to have had some compensation by now. I was just trying to fix up some private physiotherapy with a friend of mine. I'll write down her phone number and her address. You just give her a ring if you can fix anything up. Meanwhile, I'm afraid you will need to go to the hospital. Maybe your laughing policeman will be able to give you a lift,' she said saucily.

'Aye, I could do that,' Dick Ross agreed. 'I'm usually glad of something to occupy my time now that I'm on my own.'

In the face of their brisk optimism, Simon's spirits had risen slightly but as they left the hospital he heard two of the cleaning women discussing their Christmas shopping. Although it was still early December, the days were short, and the afternoon was dull and grey as Dick Ross pushed Simon's wheel-chair towards the carpark.

As they drove through the city streets, the shop windows were bright with Christmas lights and glittering decorations. Simon thought of last Christmas and felt himself sinking into the familiar pit of despondency.

He was still suffering the depressing frustration of his day in Glasgow when Roni arrived at Glendocken for their weekly session with her accounts. Her cheeks glowed from the cold, winter air, but it was anticipation which added the light to her bright brown eyes. She missed her grandfather's amiable chatter and, after spending much of her time working alone in the gardens, she looked forward to her time with the Coles. She loved the comfortable room with its cosy fire, its shaded lamps and rich, velvet curtains. In spite of the difference in their generations, she felt Ruth Cole's welcome was that of a sincere friend.

Roni was wearing a new green sweater. The emerald colour seemed to emphasise the glints in her dark hair in the gleam of a nearby lamp. She had been looking forward to the evening but even before she had finished setting out her books, she sensed Simon's dark mood. Her heart sank. She could almost feel the tension in him.

Roni felt her confidence begin to evaporate and as usual the more agitated she felt, the more mistakes she made. She thought Simon had grown used to many of her foibles, often correcting small mistakes automatically, occasionally giving her a rueful smile. Tonight was different. He was preoccupied and short-tempered. They had worked less than quarter of an hour when he suddenly flung aside his pen.

'For goodness' sake, how can we balance anything if you have sixty-one days in a month?' he exploded.

'But you know I meant the sixteenth. You know I get the numbers the wrong way round sometimes.'

'And you expect me to keep on correcting them? I'm not an infant teacher,' he snapped.

Roni stared at him helplessly, hurt and dismayed by the change in his attitude.

'I'm sorry, but . . .'

'But nothing! If you can't take the trouble to enter the figures correctly why should I try to account for a miserable patch of carrots and a bundle of mouldy old leeks!'

His scornful words shook Roni and her hurt gave way to anger. She welcomed it. It dispelled the threatening tears.

'Then don't bother!'

She snatched up the books and rose to her feet in a single swift movement. Her action took Simon by surprise.

'Please tell your mother I had to leave.'

'Hey! Wait!' he called out but Roni was already in the hall, grabbing her coat and running down the drive to her van.

How lightly, how gracefully she had moved, even in anger, Simon thought, regret and frustration battling in his brain. He screwed his eyes tightly shut but he had a mental picture of patches of angry colour on Roni's cheeks, the brilliance of her dark eyes. But before the anger, for a fleeting instant, he had glimpsed the hurt, like that of a child, slapped by a beloved mother for some crime she had not committed.

He slumped back in his wheel-chair,

shoulders hunched. Why, oh, why did he have to hurt the people he loved most? For the umpteenth time since the accident, he wished he could go to sleep and never wake up.

## CHAPTER FIVE

Roni regretted her hasty departure from Glendocken even before she reached home. She cursed her hasty flare of temper and foolish pride but she was relieved Simon had not witnessed her tears. She remembered the misery of her schooldays, her inability to finish on time, or to get things right, her frustration, the teacher's impatience, her own humiliation. Then came the outbursts of temper to camouflage her despair and inadequacy.

'Well, that's the finish!' she declared aloud as she thrust the big iron key into the lock and flung open the door of the lodge. 'I shall never, ever go near Simon Cole again, or any other teacher!'

She did not sleep well that night and awakened pale and unrefreshed.

'My word, Roni, you don't look so good this morning,' Janey French remarked with concern when she delivered her vegetables to the Silver Plume Inn.

She took the large wicker basket from Roni.

'You're not sickening for flu or anything like

that, are you? Not this near Christmas, I hope.'

'Of course not.'

'Good. Well, come and have a cup of coffee and tell Aunt Janey what's taken the sparkle out of your bonnie eyes. I've never seen you look so peaky.'

She led the way through to the large, modern kitchen and poured two mugs of steaming coffee. She took a sip or two, surveying Roni over the rim of her mug.

'I don't know about you, Roni, but I'm ready for this. Our venture into bar meals is beginning to take off at last. That's why I need the extra vegetables today.'

'I'm sure you'll soon be drawing in the crowds when people hear about your home-cooked meals,' Roni said. 'Adding on the old stone barn for a dining-room was a great idea.'

'We have that brother of mine to thank for that stroke of inspiration. Mark will be here for Christmas in ten days or so, not that he's much use when it comes to the chores. I expect he'll be more interested in your plans for the tea-room. He loves planning new ventures. I just wish he would plan his own life and settle down with a nice wife.'

'I expect he will when he's ready,' Roni said, 'but I think he would need a very meek wife who would fall in with all his ideas.'

'You do? I hope you're wrong, Roni. The wife I had in mind for him has a mind of her own and she is not at all meek and mild.'

63

'Oh, do I know her?'

Janey didn't reply directly but went on, 'Mark is really looking forward to helping you with your alterations.'

'He's in for a disappointment then. I'm not going ahead with any plans.In fact, I think I may have to look for a job. At least I can cook and . . .'

'You certainly can! I'd snatch you up in two shakes of a lamb's tail if there was enough work here to keep the two of us busy, but one day it's hectic and the next it can be dead,'

'It will get better once you build up a reputation.'

'I hope you're right. But, Roni, you would never give up the gardens, would you?'

Janey stared at her young friend incredulously.

'You love that place and you are so happy working with your plants. I've never known anyone who can make things grow like you. Tom thinks we should arrange to buy all our vegetables from you.'

'You girls talking about me?'

Janey's husband put his head round the kitchen door.

'Roni's thinking of giving up the gardens and taking a job,' Janey said with a troubled frown.

They were both genuinely fond of Roni, and Janey suspected that her brother was beginning to feel more than affection for their young friend, too.

'You've always seemed so serene. I've never seen you look so downhearted before,' Janey went on.

'Oh, I'm all right,' Roni said and summoned a smile. 'I shall keep on the gardens for this year. If they don't make enough to keep me, then I'll look for other work.'

She stood up and her lips firmed resolutely.

'Before you go, Roni, I don't suppose you can do anything to improve this Christmas wreath, can you?' Tom asked. 'Come and see. It's hanging on the front door but it looks as though the cat has mauled it. Janey only bought it yesterday.'

'Cat mauled it!' Janey echoed indignantly. 'Tom French, you know that wreath cost me eighteen pounds from Jamieson's!'

Tom grinned and ducked his head to avoid Janey's fist.

'Oh, Janey! Surely you didn't pay eighteen pounds for that!' Roni gasped when she saw it.

'Are you taking Tom's side, Veronica Kennedy?' Janey chuckled good-naturedly. 'It does look rather bedraggled, doesn't it?'

'Just a bit,' Roni replied ruefully. 'Granny used to make a wreath every Christmas, to hang on our door at the lodge.'

'I know. That's what gave me the idea. It always seemed so welcoming. Could you do anything with this one?'

'I could try. I have loads of fir cones and

holly at the lodge. I'd rather have a go at making one from scratch though, before I start pulling yours to bits. It does seem rather insecure.'

'I know Tom's right,' Janey agreed, 'but I did want to get this Christmas off to a good start.'

'I've none of those shiny baubles and ribbons, though,' Roni pointed out.

'I have,' Janey interrupted eagerly. 'We have a whole box of bits and bobs left over from the decorations. Take the lot. They're no use to us. Do say you'll have a go, Roni, if only to stop this man of mine getting at me every time he sees it.'

She squeezed her husband's arm affectionately. Roni always felt warmed in their presence, as well as being grateful for their increasing vegetable orders.

She stayed up late that night wiring the cones she had collected. There was an abundance of fresh greenery along her part of the drive and all around the gardens and she had no difficulty selecting holly with plenty of berries. She added a few shiny red baubles to please Janey's more flamboyant taste.

Both Janey and Tom were delighted with the wreath when Roni delivered it but she refused their generous offer of payment.

'I shall find a way to repay you, Roni,' Janey said, rapturous as a child in her delight. 'Here, take this monstrosity out of my sight. You might be able to salvage some of the ribbons to make a wreath for your own front door.'

Janey looked keenly at the shadows beneath Roni's big brown eyes.

'You do know you're welcome to spend Christmas with us, don't you, darling girl? The trouble is, it looks like being almost too hectic. We're nearly fully booked for Christmas dinners so you'd probably end up helping.'

'Don't you worry about me,' Roni reassured her quickly. 'To tell the truth I hadn't really thought about Christmas until you asked me to make the wreath. I will take this away though and make one for the lodge, or maybe Jugs would like one for his mother. He comes every Saturday now, more often if he has time off from college. He got the chance of an old scooter and he has done it up. He's a great help.'

\*      \*      \*

Roni felt rather proud of her efforts as she stepped back to survey the door of the lodge, now transformed by a festive garland. Almost as good as Granny used to make, she thought with a smile. Now that she had the knack of it, it took very little time to make another wreath ready for Jugs, but before she had finished adding the final touches, the telephone rang.

'Hi, Roni!' Janey's exuberant voice came over. 'I've a big favour to ask you. You know the wreath you made for our front door?'

'Surely it hasn't come to pieces as well!'

'Oh, no! As soon as he saw it, Jim Shaw, one of our regulars, asked if I could get one like it for his wife. He was admiring it again on his way out when we had a visit from Mr and Mrs Grant, you know the couple who moved into that big white house at the top of the hill?'

'Garner Mount? I do indeed. You must be going really upmarket, Janey!' Roni teased.

'Would you believe this then? They want to book a lunch party for fourteen for Boxing Day.'

'We hadn't meant to, but we can't refuse an order like that, can we? Anyway, Mrs Grant got her eye on your wreath as well and she asked if I could get two for her. Could you manage to make them, Roni?'

Janey's voice sounded anxious now.

'I know the Grants would pay you well if you can find time. I thought you'd be able to manage one for Jimmy Shaw's wife so I'd already told him it would be sixteen pounds. He said that was fine and his wife would be really pleased. I never thought of the Grants wanting to buy two.'

'Sixteen pounds! You're charging sixteen pounds for a wreath?' Roni asked in astonishment.

'I'm not, but you are. You can't make them for nothing. There's time and skill involved, as well as materials. Anyway, that's two pounds cheaper than Jamieson's. The question is, will you have time to make two for the Grants as well as Jim's?'

'I'll make time at that price.'

It was the following afternoon when Roni recognised Ruth Cole's car drawing between the sandstone pillars into the drive. Roni had been feeling guilty about the way she had left Ruth's home. She went out to meet her.

'I hope you don't mind me calling, Roni.'

Ruth's face was strained and she looked tired.

'No, of course not,' Roni replied, feeling the colour rush to her cheeks as she remembered her hasty departure two nights ago. 'It was rude of me to rush away without saying goodbye.'

'Please, don't apologise, my dear,' Ruth interrupted. 'I do need some fresh vegetables, but I did hope you might have time for a little chat.'

'Of course. You will have to excuse the litter but I have been making up wreaths for an order.'

'Oh, yes! I see them. Is that one on your own door? They are lovely, really lovely. I had no idea you could do things like that.'

'Neither had I.'

Roni busied herself putting the kettle on to the cooker to boil and setting out a tray of home-made biscuits.

'I helped Gran often enough, then Janey

French asked me to make one for the Silver Plume and she got orders for more.'

Roni paused. She knew she was chattering nervously.

'Roni, I really am sorry you had to leave the other night,' Ruth said quietly but there was a note of desperation in her voice. 'Simon was reluctant to go back to the hospital in Glasgow and I expect he was tired after the journey, but that can never excuse his black moods and sharp tongue. He must have hurt you badly to make you leave so suddenly.'

'He'd been at the hospital? I had no idea. I wouldn't have troubled him if I'd known.'

'Something must have upset him. He seemed to be enjoying the book-keeping sessions with you. Joseph and I have been surprised at the interest he has taken. He asked me to get him some gardening books from the library a fortnight ago.'

'Oh, he never mentioned that.'

'No, he keeps too much to himself these days. He has hardly spoken since his visit to the hospital. I keep wondering if he got a bad report but Joseph doesn't think it could have been that because the nurse says his leg has almost healed and he ought to be having more physiotherapy. Mr Ross, the man who chauffeured him to Glasgow, arrived this afternoon and he has persuaded Simon to go for a drive. I don't know where but I got the impression he had a definite purpose.'

'I see,' Roni said. 'No wonder Simon was tired of me and my mistakes if his own day had been such an ordeal.'

'So you will come as usual next week, dear? Please?' Ruth said.

Roni hesitated.

'I don't think it's a good idea. I must stop pestering him with my accounts. In fact, I've decided to stop doing them altogether.'

Roni was surprised to see real disappointment in the older woman's eyes.

'Oh, my dear, Roni! Can you manage to prepare the figures yourself now?'

'No, and I never shall be able to manage such things. There would never be an end to them either, with accounts for accepting a grant, for taxes, for employing someone to help.'

She shook her head.

'I've been thinking about it, and I know now I don't really want to build on a tea-room anyway. This is my home. I should never have listened to Mark's ideas. If the gardens will not support me I shall look for a job as a cook.'

'It seems a pity to give up all your plans. Your heart is in gardening.'

'Yes. I can't imagine living anywhere but here. I would hate to give it up.'

'I can understand how you feel. It's so quiet and peaceful, and so pleasant being able to walk down to the river.'

'Yes. When I was small, Grandfather was

71

still employed up at Bellingdale House, but we used to keep ducks and bantams on the ground beside the river. I loved going every day to feed them. In the spring, Gran set eggs for hatching. The chicks were so beautiful.'

She stopped suddenly, her eyes widening.

'I've just had an idea!'

'A good one by the look on your face.'

Ruth smiled with real affection.

'Well, it might be worth a try. I was telling you about the Silver Plume. Tom and Janey French are aiming at quality food and Tom thinks it might be a good idea to source organic produce such as my fresh vegetables, so that they can market it as an added attraction. If it proves successful, maybe they could use free range eggs as well, don't you think?'

'And you plan to supply them?'

'No?' Roni asked in disappointment. 'You think it's a stupid idea?'

'Oh, no, I don't think that, Roni! I'm just amazed that you have so much courage and enthusiasm. You would be a proper young businesswoman if you had the capital to carry out all your ideas.'

'I would need enough profit to pay someone to keep accounts for me,' Roni reminded her. 'Anyway, I will see what Jugs can do. We still have two small henhouses amongst the trees but they would need some repairs.'

'Jugs? Is that the student from the college?

72

Does he still come to help?'

'Oh, yes, he's a good worker, and quite clever with his hands. I think some of his mates resent him spending his time here though, instead of with the gang. He said they had tried to follow him a fortnight ago. He made several detours and managed to shake them off. I hope they don't persuade him to stop coming.'

'I hope they don't follow him here either!' Ruth said in alarm. 'It is very isolated for a girl to live alone.'

'Yes, but I'm used to it and I don't mind it being quiet. In fact, I love it. I can't imagine wanting to live anywhere else. Even if Jugs' cronies did come they'd soon lose interest when they see there is no entertainment for them. I'm amazed that Jugs has kept on coming.'

'I heard Joseph and Andrew Woodward discussing your young protégé. Apparently his attendance and his work at the college have improved tremendously this term. They think it is because he has broken away from his crowd. Most of them seem to have dropped out of their courses or given up any employment they ever had.'

'I'm glad. I just wish I could afford to pay him instead of just giving him his food. He says his mother wouldn't know how to cook vegetables out of a garden when I offered him some. I have baked and decorated a Christmas

73

cake for him to take home to his young sister. I hope she will like it.'

Roni's voice tailed off uncertainly as she brought the cake from the pantry which opened off the kitchen. She looked anxiously at Ruth's face, seeing the surprise in her eyes.

'My dear Roni, you've made an excellent job. I love the little sugar angels, and the crib with the baby. Where did you get the Christmas roses on the sides. Did you buy them?'

'Oh, no. I couldn't afford to buy them,' Roni said regretfully. 'I copied some of them from an old magazine.'

'I had no idea you were so artistic!'

Roni flushed with pleasure and her eyes brightened.

'Gran used to say I was artistic, too. She said I took after my mother because I love painting, and she did, too. Her books are all I have of her. Would you like to see them?'

'Oh, yes, please.'

Ruth was thoroughly intrigued and when Roni returned, she had three small watercolour paintings as well as the books.

'These illustrations are beautiful! They're so real they almost grow out of the page,' Ruth said, turning one page after another. 'And these, too.'

She picked up two of the paintings.

'Winter, summer and autumn. They are delightful.'

She turned and glanced out of the window.

'Isn't that the view from the window?'

'Yes, I painted it as I remembered it last winter.'

'You painted these yourself?'

'The art teacher at school was the only one I ever seemed to please.'

'It's a pity to keep them hidden in a drawer.'

Roni looked back at Ruth and an idea crystallised in her mind. Jugs had mentioned the college did picture framing for the price of the materials. Now she had money from the sale of the wreaths, she could have them framed as gifts, if Jugs could get them done in time.

'To tell the truth,' Ruth said, 'I really came to ask if you will go with me to the carol service on Christmas Eve. Simon nearly always came, but this year everything is changed.'

Roni saw her mouth tremble, but Ruth pulled herself together.

'I hate the thought of leaving him on his own on Christmas Eve and I know Joseph is quite happy to stay at home, too.'

'I'd love to come with you,' Roni said.

'It would be even better if you would come home with me afterwards. Would you stay overnight and join us for Christmas dinner?'

Roni caught her breath, then she expelled it slowly, her eyes fixed intently on the older woman's wistful face.

'I think you are trying to do me a favour.

You know this will be the first Christmas I have been on my own. I am truly grateful for your invitation, but I couldn't possibly stay at Glendocken. I vowed I would never trouble Simon again.'

'But, my dear, whatever Simon said, I'm sure he didn't mean to hurt you so badly. What is more,' she added firmly, 'Glendocken is my home, too, ands don't want you to stay away. I love Simon dearly, but he is not a child. He used to be so considerate.'

'You're very kind. I will go with you to church, and I truly appreciate your invitation to stay with you over Christmas, but . . .'

She trembled, remembering Simon's scornful voice.

'There's plenty of time. Just think about it and let me know. I'm convinced it is good for Simon to have young company. Anyway, I don't like the thought of you spending Christmas here on your own.'

'Please, don't worry. Janey has already invited me over to the Silver Plume if I feel lonely. I shall probably be too tired to do anything but sleep. There are always extra deliveries to do the day before Christmas.'

'Yes. I had better collect my vegetables now and let you get on with your work.'

'I'll just get them for you,' Roni offered.

Ruth admired her as she ran down the path and vaulted over the low fence which divided the vegetable plots from the lodge's flowerbeds. She sighed, remembering how Simon had once moved like lightning on the football pitch and the badminton court. Now he could barely haul himself to the bathroom without help.

No wonder he is so bitter, she thought with a heavy heart. I vow I'll do everything in my power to help him.

'Are you feeling all right?' Roni asked anxiously as she returned, seeing her closed eyes and pale, strained face.

'Yes! Yes, thank you, dear. I'd better hurry home now. I expect Simon will have returned.'

## CHAPTER SIX

Ruth had been home more than a couple of hours. She had cooked the evening meal and Joseph had enjoyed a pre-dinner drink, but still there was no sign of Dick Ross, the driver, and Simon.

'They can't be driving around the countryside for pleasure. It is pitch black outside and it's freezing,' Joseph said at last.

'Dinner is ready. Do you want to start, dear?'

Joseph shook his head. Neither of them felt like eating.

'That's a car in the drive now!'

He hurried to the window and Ruth realised

he was just as anxious and tense about Simon as she was herself. Even before Dick Ross had manoeuvred Simon and his wheel-chair into the room, Ruth sensed their air of excitement. She couldn't believe it.

'Have you enough dinner for an extra one, Mother?' Simon asked cheerfully.

'I could easily stretch to another.'

She smiled at Dick Ross.

'I don't want to intrude, Mrs Cole,' Dick Ross said, 'but Simon has been telling me what an excellent cook you are.'

'He has?'

Ruth glanced at her son in surprise. She had tried so hard to tempt his appetite but he had found fault with almost everything since he came home from hospital.

'You know you are, Mum, so don't fish for compliments.'

Simon grinned at her and Ruth felt her heart leap with gratitude to see a glimpse of the old teasing Simon.

An hour later, Dick Ross eased back his chair and patted his stomach.

'That was delicious. It's years since I tasted home-made lentil soup, and I haven't had a beef casserole since my wife died.'

'You're more than welcome, Mr Ross,' Ruth said as she passed a steaming cup of coffee, 'anytime.'

He nodded, knowing she was silently thanking him for helping her son.

'Aren't you going to tell your parents what you've been up to today, Simon?' he said.

'Maybe it would be better to wait until we have some definite news,' Simon suggested. 'I don't want to raise false hopes.'

'I think they deserve some hope after all they've been through. Simon tells me you gave up your job to look after him, Mrs Cole.'

'Yes, but I was just thankful he was alive. We both were.'

'Well, nothing can put his leg back, I know that,' Dick Ross sympathised, 'but if he had been my son, I'd get him anything which might help him back to a normal life.'

'It is what we would like, too, Mr Ross,' Joseph said a little stiffly, 'but I'm sure you'll agree that's easier said than done.'

'Dick has been making enquiries on my behalf with a couple of lawyers, Father, and he's managed to sift out some information from the police. It seems I may be able to get some sort of compensation if we get a good lawyer.'

'Yes, dear, I'm sure you will, but it could take years to make a successful claim. I didn't want you raising more false hopes,' Ruth said.

'I don't think it will be years, Mrs Cole,' Dick Ross contradicted gently. 'Simon was convinced the boys from his youth club must have witnessed the accident so I decided to see some of them myself. Sure enough, two of the lads had a good description of the car, including part of the number plate. One of them had seen the occupants. Apparently the senior of the two policemen who took statements from the lads dismissed them as malicious lies. The only car they could trace which came anywhere near their description belonged to a well-known businessman who owns a string of garages. He and his wife are both public figures and they do a lot for charity. They have one son and he is at boarding school.'

'Thanks to Dick,' Simon said jubilantly, 'he persuaded some of my lads to accompany him to the police station again. Their statements were exactly the same as before.'

He looked triumphant.

'I'm sure your lads were telling the truth, Simon,' Ruth said cautiously, 'but don't get your hopes too high.'

'Don't worry, Mum. They told Dick they had tried to visit me in hospital. The first time, I was still unconscious, but even when they went back a second time the staff wouldn't let them into see me.'

He grinned his old boyish grin. Ruth's heart gave a leap of joy to see the light back in his eyes.

'Their language could be pretty rough at times,' he admitted ruefully, 'but it's worth more than any compensation just to know they wanted to see me. They really cared, really did want to help me. The third time they were told

I'd been moved, and here I was, believing they'd forgotten me.'

'And help they have,' Dick said. 'Their story has never varied and the police are now making further investigations.'

'Thanks to Dick's persistence,' Simon said. 'I can't tell you how grateful I am to you for going to the club and seeing the lads, Dick.'

'I'm glad I went. I like to see justice done. The man who is inspector now is a keen young fellow. He'll haul somebody over the coals for not following up the enquiry at the time.'

'Do they know who owned the car then?' Joseph asked.

'They are still making further enquiries, Mr Cole, but there were traces of blue paint on the wall where the car mounted the kerb and it matches a car owned by a Mr Gordon Campbell of Campbell and Carsewood Motors.'

'I've heard of them,' Joseph Cole exclaimed. 'That's a big concern. I've seen adverts on television. They are into all sorts of things to do with cars and small commercial vehicles.'

'Indeed they are, but they started off as a small family business. A brother and sister married a brother and sister so the two partners are brothers-in-law. They and their wives were away for a long weekend in Paris at the time of Simon's accident. Both their sons were at their boarding school, or supposed to be.'

Joseph sat up straighter.

'The boys knew their parents were away and hitched a lift home. Campbell's son, George, is fifteen and desperate to leave school and get started in the garage, but his parents want him to be educated. His cousin, William Carsewood, is a year younger. Apparently they went for a spot of joy-riding in the Campbell's limousine. They got lost and ended up in an area of the city which was totally unfamiliar. It is pretty rough round about the Baillie Boys' Club, isn't it, Simon?'

'It is, rather.' Simon nodded. 'Half of them have never had a chance of a normal life. They're not bad lads when you get to know them, it's just that they have their own rules, their own code of honour. A fancy limousine and two well-dressed lads would stick out like a sore thumb. I expect they both panicked.'

'Yes,' Dick Ross agreed, 'and these two boys have led extremely sheltered lives, but nothing excuses what they did. After they'd found their way back home and returned the car they high-tailed it back to their school. Their parents never knew they'd been away. The car was not all that badly damaged considering what they did to Simon. One wing had been grazed on the sandstone gatepost at the entrance to their home. Whether or not that was coincidence we don't know. The foreman at the garage automatically got it repaired ready for Campbell's return.'

'But surely they must have read about the accident in the newspapers,' Ruth said.

'Yes, and the boys realised they were responsible, but they didn't own up. It has affected them badly apparently. They haven't been able to concentrate on their work and they've been given medical checks because they weren't eating, and couldn't sleep. I expect it's nerves. I reckon they might be relieved the whole business has been brought into the open though goodness knows how they'll face the consequences.'

'Their parents must be distraught,' Ruth said slowly.

'Yes, so I believe. Simon should have no problem getting compensation though. Some of it should be paid before very long, I think. The inspector who is handling the case now says Mr Campbell is keen to avoid as much publicity as he can. I'm not too well informed on that side of things. My job was to catch the people responsible. We left the legal matters to the courts and lawyers.'

'It could ruin the boys' lives if they have to go to a young offenders' institution and mix with hardened young criminals,' Simon said with a troubled frown.

'Their actions have turned your life upside down, Simon,' his father pointed out. 'They have to be punished.'

'The Chief Inspector has met Campbell's wife at several charity functions. He says she is blaming herself for giving too much attention to her charity work and not enough to her own son. It must have been a shock to her.'

'It was a shock to us. They nearly killed Simon.'

Ruth sounded near to tears.

'Nearly,' Simon agreed with a new acceptance which surprised both his parents, 'but not quite. So don't upset yourself, Mother. The really good news to come out of all this is that my lads hadn't deserted me, as I thought. I must have had some influence on them after all and it has restored my faith in human nature. We should thank Dick for doing a good job of sleuthing.'

Dick waved aside their gratitude.

'Sometimes it's hard to remember I'm supposed to be retired. Tell your parents about our other bit of work today, Simon.'

'Oh, yes. We went to see the physiotherapist. She's going to start treatment right away. She says she will wait for her pay until I get the compensation.'

'That's very generous! Trusting, too,' Ruth said.

'It is,' Joseph agreed gruffly, 'but we'll see she gets paid right away, even if we have to take out a mortgage again.'

'We owe you more than we realised, Mr Ross.'

'Do call me Dick, please. And there's no need to thank me. I'm really glad to help and I reckon Simon will take the hurdles in his stride.'

He caught the glint of laughter in Simon's eyes at his choice of words.

'Eh, I didn't mean . . .'

He wagged a finger at Simon's quirky smile.

'You'll not recognise yourself by this time next year.'

'I hope you're right,' Simon said soberly, but the shadows were fleeting.

Ruth was relieved to see the faint smile return. It was the best Christmas gift they could have had. At least Simon had hope again. He was young and there was a lot of life ahead.

\*　　　\*　　　\*

Jugs was speechless when Roni showed him the Christmas garland she had made for his mother, but then was almost overcome when she showed him the Christmas cake. He turned away, but not before she had seen the look of awe and an unexpected glint of tears.

'We never had a Christmas cake before,' he told her gruffly as he fumbled in his pocket for a non-existent tissue.

Failing to find one he gave an enormous sniff and then another, dragged the back of his hand across his eyes and turned to face her.

'I haven't got a present for you,' he said slowly.

'These are not presents either, Jugs. They are just things I've made myself. They are a poor return for all the work you've done for me, and there's a whole lot more to do if you are going to keep on coming, but I still have no money to pay you properly. I only wish I had.'

She then went on to tell him of her plans to renovate the two huts to keep some chickens. His eyes lit up with as much excitement as if she had given him a treasure. Roni grinned back at him.

'This will be the best Christmas me and our Emma have ever had.'


## CHAPTER SEVEN

On Christmas Eve, Roni and Jugs worked steadily, their fingers throbbing with the raw dampness of the December morning, their backs aching from bending over the vegetable plots. Eventually they wheeled the vegetables into one of the sheds for weighing and packing.

'Come on, Jugs, we'll have a bowl of hot soup.'

'But it's not lunchtime yet! We've all these to weigh up. Then you've to deliver them.'

'I know, but it will warm us up. Listen, is that the phone? Come on.'

She sped across the drive to the house and

reached the phone before the ringing stopped.

'Thank goodness I've got you at last!' Janey's voice gasped over the wires. 'I've been trying and trying. Where have you been, Roni?'

'Pulling sprouts and cutting cabbages and broccoli,' Roni said wearily. 'And there's more to do yet so . . .'

'So, I want you to double my order for sprouts!'

Janey's voice was a mixture of triumph and anxiety.

'Double it! Janey, I don't know if I can.'

'Oh, Roni, you must. I'm relying on you. We've had nine last-minute bookings.'

'But I thought you were full up.'

'We are!' Janey wailed. 'It was Mark who took them this morning. Never turn anyone away, he says! Never mind that I shall have to sit them on the mantelshelf.'

'Oh, Janey.'

Roni couldn't suppress a slight chuckle at the prospect of several large figures perched on the oak beam which was supposed to add an air of olde worlde charm to the new dining-room of the Silver Plume!

'So how are you going to fit them in?' she asked seriously.

'You might well ask! Mark and Tom are busy improvising a screen to partition off part of the bar lounge then Mark is coming over to collect the vegetables. Don't keep him talking.

I've told him he has to prepare them, if he is going to claim a share of the profits, but you know my brother! Mark thinks chores are for other people. This is our biggest break, though, since we did the renovations. If I didn't know how busy you are I would ask you to come and help, Roni.'

'Sorry . . . ah, there's a car. Cheerio, Janey, and good luck.'

Roni replaced the receiver with a sigh. She didn't know how she could fit in all the work she had to do.

After a hasty lunch, Roni delivered the vegetables they had ready while Jugs went to pick some more. When she returned, they worked on in silence, too tired to talk. Eventually the fading light forced them to stop.

'I will make a cup of tea and a sandwich before you go, Jugs. The roads will be icy soon. And I must get this lot to Mr Johnstone, the greengrocer over at Pendon.'

'There's still four boxes of vegetables in the sorting shed,' Jugs reminded her. 'Have you forgotten to take one of the orders?'

Roni peered into the shed.

'Oh, no! These are for the Silver Plume! Mark Houston was supposed to be collecting them hours ago.'

It was dark and a raw mist had descended by the time Roni had completed all her deliveries. The forecast was for a clear, frosty night but the freezing fog had persisted all day. She was tired, hungry and longing for a long, hot bath to ease her aching muscles. When she drew into the tree-lined drive, her heartbeat quickened in alarm at the sight of two red tail lights gleaming in the darkness. Then she recognised Mark Houston's silhouette in the glare of her headlights.

'Did you forget to call earlier?' she greeted him. 'I'll bet Janey was cross when you arrived back without the vegetables.'

'I didn't forget. I had lunch with an old friend. The time just drifted away. You know how it is.'

'I wish I did!'

'Well, you're back now. I knew if I waited you'd help me with the vegetables. Shall we do them here or do you want to come back to the Silver Plume and do them?'

'You're not serious! Anyway, I thought you were supposed to be helping Tom behind the bar this evening.'

He clapped a dramatic hand to his forehead.

'It slipped my mind. Never mind, I expect you'll manage to do the veggies without me.'

Roni almost flung the sprouts at him.

'Mark Houston, I am cold, tired and hungry. All you've done is laze around and chat. If you think I'm going to help you now you can think again! The least you can do is give Janey some support. It takes more than ideas and money to build up a business, you know.'

'Why, Roni! I didn't know you had such a temper. You're really attractive with the colour in your cheeks.'

Before Roni realised his intention, he bent and kissed her hard on the mouth. Shock kept her still until his embrace tightened then she pushed him away so violently he almost lost his balance.

'Come on, Roni. What's a kiss between friends? It is Christmas after all.'

'Well, it doesn't feel like it to me. Take those other two boxes to your car, now! I'm going to put the light off and lock up. Then I'm going to have a long soak in a hot bath.'

Mark gazed at her. He had never seen Roni lose her temper. It had never occurred to him she would refuse to prepare the vegetables. He stared in disbelief as she walked away and closed the lodge door firmly behind her.

As Roni lay soaking in her bath a little while later, she had time to reflect on the day's events. She felt a little ashamed of losing her temper but she had been exhausted, and exasperated with Mark. She remembered his kiss and rubbed her mouth. Janey and Tom were good friends. She would hate to lose them and she prayed that everything would be a success for their first big Christmas venture at the Silver Plume.

When Ruth called to collect Roni to go to the carol service, her earlier exhaustion had vanished. She had opened the blouse which Janey had bought her for Christmas. She had known Janey was buying her a blouse because she had asked her size, but she had not expected anything so lovely. It was an emerald green silky material with a mandarin collar and tiny loops to fasten the neat, shell buttons.

The only suitable skirt she had was a fine wool, full-skirted, black one, plain but stylish. She put it on and slipped her arms into the blouse. It felt wonderful against her warm skin. She made a little pirouette in front of the mirror, pleased and happy. On impulse she decided to coil her hair up on top of her head.

Ruth exclaimed in admiration when she arrived to collect her.

'My dear, you look lovely, and so absolutely right for Christmas, too. I love your hair in that style. It suits you perfectly, especially with that stand-up collar. I'm really pleased you've agreed to spend Christmas with us after all, Roni, dear.'

'Thank you.'

The little church was a mile from the village, perched on a hillside, and lights from the arched stone windows gleamed warmly on the frosted path and gravestones. The mist had cleared and the sky looked like a gold-studded velvet curtain with the twinkling stars and almost a full moon.

The church filled up and soon the strains of old, familiar carols echoed around its rafters as voices rose in joyous praise.

As midnight struck, the main lights were dimmed and an expectant hush descended. The only light came from small lanterns held by the choir and the advent candles, mellowing the ancient stonework, flickering flames gleaming and reflecting the rich colours of the stained glass window above the attar. Softly the organist began to play *Silent Night*. There was a lump in Roni's throat but she felt a wonderful peace and tranquillity. As the last chords died away, she met Ruth Cole's glance and smiled.

'Thank you for asking me,' she said quietly. 'It was a beautiful service.'

'Thank you for coming, Roni.' Ruth smiled warmly. 'A happy Christmas, to you, my dear.'

Joseph had the kettle boiling and a plate of warmed mince pies ready for them when they returned.

'You waited up then, Simon?' Ruth said in surprise seeing her son there, too. 'I thought you would be tired.'

'Not as tired as Roni, I'll bet. Anyway I wanted to wish you both a happy Christmas.'

'Thank you, dear.'

Ruth smiled and bent to kiss him.

'And may you have many happy Christmases to enjoy.'

'Only time will tell. Come on, Veronica, aren't you going to wish me happy Christmas, too?'

His smile was infectious and Roni took his outstretched hand. She was surprised when he drew her down towards him and kissed her firmly on the mouth. She knew the ready colour was rising in her cheeks but she said softly, 'Happy Christmas, Simon.'

He grinned up at her.

'I do believe it might be after all.'

His eyes danced mischievously and Roni could not help smiling back.

'You look very lovely tonight,' he said, and Roni glimpsed the wistful look in his eyes and wondered if he was remembering other Christmases and the beautiful girls who had probably been his companions.

They were just finishing their tea and mince pies when the sound of the doorbell startled them. It was loud and persistent. Joseph Cole answered the urgent summons. Roni stared as he returned, followed by Mark Houston. She had never seen Janey's suave brother so agitated, his hair dishevelled and his face pale and drawn.

'Roni! Thank goodness I've found you at last!'

'Is something wrong?'

She was dismayed that he had thrust himself into the Coles' home. He was not normally so rude.

'It's Janey. She's in hospital.'

'Janey? Oh, no! Why? What has happened?'

'You'll say it's my fault,' he groaned. 'I

didn't tell her I hadn't prepared the vegetables until the middle of the evening. She was even more angry than you were. In fact, she burst into tears. I've never seen Janey cry before, not over something so trivial.'

'Trivial! It's terribly important to Janey to make a success tomorrow.'

Flags of angry colour stained Roni's cheeks. She was oblivious now to the three Coles watching them.

'Why is Janey in hospital?'

'She was lifting a roast from the oven. She was tense and tired and maybe she wasn't concentrating. I don't know. Anyway, the hot fat went all over her hand and arm and down her thigh to her ankle.'

'Oh, no! Poor girl.'

Ruth Cole echoed Roni's gasp.

'Tom went with her to the hospital. I managed the bar on my own.'

'What about Janey?' Roni asked impatiently. 'How bad is she?'

'Pretty bad, I reckon. They are keeping her in on account of the shock, as well as the burns. Tom said they had given her an injection for the pain and to make her sleep. Roni, we need you desperately. You're the only one who can help us save the Silver Plume. Will you help? Please, Roni, if only for Janey's sake, come with me now.'

'Now!' Ruth Cole exclaimed, and crossed to Roni's side protectively. 'Young man, have you any idea what a long and arduous day this poor girl has had?'

'Well, what else can I do?' Mark muttered querulously. 'No-one else would turn out to help at this late stage and the hotel is booked solid for tomorrow's Christmas dinners. Janey had a list of things to do as long as my arm and she was only halfway down it.'

'I must go,' Roni said as she turned to Ruth with a troubled face. 'I must help, for Janey's sake. She has been a very good friend to me. I know how much this Christmas means to her and Tom.'

'But you must get some sleep first, Roni! You are tired out before you start,' Ruth protested anxiously. 'That's when accidents happen.'

'Mother is right.'

They were all surprised by Simon's intervention.

'I suggest we all get a few hours' sleep, then I will come with you to the Silver Plume. I can peel potatoes and chop up carrots.'

'You're really willing to help? Oh, thank you, Simon.'

Roni spun round and gave him a spontaneous hug of gratitude. He clasped one of her hands and their eyes met.

'Thank you,' he said quietly, 'for not putting obstacles in my way just because I'm in a wheel-chair.'

'I don't think of the wheel-chair as an

obstacle to preparing vegetables, or anything else. It's more a case of being willing to get on with it.'

She turned to Mark.

'Isn't that right?'

'I suppose so.' Mark said heavily. 'I certainly wish I had done as Janey asked.'

'Well, it is too late for regrets now,' Ruth said briskly. 'I'm more than willing to lend a hand in the kitchen, Roni, if you can make use of me.'

'Then I'll come, too,' Joseph announced cheerfully. 'I can lay tables and help with the drinks. I worked in a hotel for two summers when I was a student but there's some things you never forget. What do you say, young man?'

'I shall be eternally grateful if we can get through tomorrow without too many complaints, and I know Janey and Tom will thank you from the bottom of their hearts.'

'It's Christmas Day already,' Ruth reminded them all. 'We should all snatch some sleep.'

\*      \*      \*

A month earlier, Ruth Cole had been dreading Christmas and Roni had not allowed herself to think about her first Christmas alone at the lodge, alone in the world, with neither kith nor kin. Yet, here they were, after one of the busiest days either could remember, enjoying a

96

belated Christmas dinner in the private living-room of the Silver Plume.

'You coped splendidly, Roni,' Ruth said as they reflected on the day's events.

'I couldn't have done it without your help, everyone's help.'

She smiled, looking around the table at Joseph, Simon, Mark and Tom.

'Janey is so methodical, too. It was just a case of working through her list. Did you tell her that, Tom?' she asked. 'I did,' Tom answered. 'She had been fretting all day.'

'Did you tell her I'm resigning from the business, Tom?' Mark asked. 'You can keep my share as an interest-free loan for as long as you need it.'

'I don't think it will be long before the Silver Plume has a fine reputation, judging by some of the comments I overheard today,' Simon said.

'Ha, yes,' Ruth nodded. 'You seemed to be enjoying yourself. I thought I recognised two of the lads who used to be at school with you.'

'Yes. It was good to chat about old times. Bill and Harry have invited me to join them for a drink one evening soon. They are going to pick me up, but they seem to take it for granted that I shall be driving myself again soon.'

'You will. Cars can be adapted to suit everyone these days,' Mark said.

'That depends on if I get enough

compensation to buy a car. Meanwhile I shall be happy if I can stand on my one good leg and get myself into a vehicle without help. One step at a time and all that.'

Simon's expression was a half-grimace, half-grin.

'Oh, I quite forgot!' Ruth said suddenly. 'We never opened our Christmas presents and we never gave you yours, Roni, dear. You must stay with us again tonight. We will open them as soon as we get home.'

Roni was too tired to argue, even if she had wanted to.

Roni still felt her three pictures were quite inadequate as gifts, in spite of the beautifully-polished frames made by the college Art Department, so she was cheered when Ruth and Joseph exclaimed with genuine pleasure over their respective pictures of summer and autumn. Only Simon remained silent, examining his picture of winter heathers and snowdrops, amidst a lingering patch of snow. There was a tiny clump of yellow celandines nestling in one corner with the red stems of the dogwood pointing up to the frosty blue sky in the background.

It was much less colourful than the summer flower border, or the burst of golden rod and crimson dahlias of autumn, but it was her favourite. She had not realised she had been holding her breath until Simon looked up and smiled.

'You really are very talented, Veronica Kennedy. I shall appreciate this painting as long as I live. It will remind me there is life and colour, if I look for it, even during the bleakest times of the year, or of life.'

'Oh, that was not my intention!' Roni gasped in dismay.

'No, I know. I can see you love painting. It is there in the detail, the light and shade, everything. But it is a lesson I shall remember and I shall treasure this picture always. Thank you.'

Roni thanked Ruth and Joseph for the beautifully-illustrated book of garden plants. Then she turned her attention to the small parcel which Simon had given her. She was surprised that he had bothered at all but she drew a breath of delight when the plain silver paper fell away to reveal a hair clasp. It was made from mother-of-pearl and fashioned in the shape of a butterfly. The wings and the body were a delicate tracery in gold and the gold antennae were each tipped with a tiny diamond. She turned to Ruth, assuming she had chosen the gift on Simon's behalf.

'It's lovely,' she said sincerely. 'How can I ever thank you?'

'Don't thank me, dear. Simon must have chosen it himself, though when and where I don't know.'

Roni was holding the clasp on top of her head, her pleasure plain to see. She turned to

Simon in surprise.

'Simon? Then I thank you twice over, for taking trouble to choose a gift for me, as well as for the gift itself.'

Ruth was sure she had glimpsed a rare tenderness in her son's eyes before he lowered them from Roni's bright gaze.

'It really is pretty, Simon, and so right for Roni, especially when she puts up her hair. But when did you go shopping?'

'Dear Mother.' Simon sighed. 'I have to do some things for myself.'

'I know, and I'm glad, but you have had so little opportunity.'

'I was waiting for Dick to collect some papers one afternoon. He parked in front of an antique shop and the hair clasp was in the centre of a tray of brooches and rings. I thought of Roni's abundant dark hair. I asked Dick to go in and buy it.'

\*         \*         \*

As January gave way to February, there were several bright sunny days reminding everyone that spring was just around the corner, but they were interspersed with bleak, grey days of sleet, and bitter winds, warning that winter was not over.

Simon co-operated with Claudia Black, his physiotherapist, and pushed himself to the limit but he felt the results were as erratic as the weather. There was no word from the police, or mention of compensation to buy a car, and his continuing dependence on his parents caused more frustration.

Roni spent days cleaning seed trays and preparing for spring sowings, digging the ground and erecting cloches to warm the soil, or working in the greenhouses. Jugs helped at every opportunity. Dick Ross had fallen into the habit of calling once or twice a week. He seemed to enjoy walking round the grounds and sometimes he stayed to help prune the fruit bushes which were beginning to grow wild in the main grounds. Roni guessed he was lonely without his wife and the regular work routine of the police force.

One evening, when she had taken Ruth's weekly vegetable order and joined the family for a meal, Simon asked, 'When is Mrs Boyd from the Enterprise Trust coming back to see you?'

His question took Roni by surprise and her cheeks flushed.

'I told her I have changed my mind about the tea-room project.'

'Oh, Roni,' Simon said, exasperated. 'You know I would have done the accounts for you. I enjoyed having something useful to do.'

'Did you?'

Roni's brows rose sceptically.

'Yes, I did. I assumed you didn't want my help and I couldn't blame you after the way I vented my frustration on you.'

'It wasn't just the accounts, or all the regulations.'

Simon would never understand how much her lack of education troubled her. He found it all so easy. To her it made an unbridgeable gulf between her and the world, and especially between her and Simon. His mind was so alert, his brain so quick. One day he would learn to walk again. He would mix with his own circle of friends and enjoy their debates and learning. But there were no such things as artificial brains.

'What was it then?' he continued.

'An extension would have spoiled the character and the peace of the lodge. It is my home and . . .'

Glancing up, she noticed that her little pictures had disappeared from their place on the living-room wall at Glendocken. True, they were small but she had painted them lovingly. She felt hurt that they had been banished already, stuffed away like the old Christmas cards.

Depression stayed with her as she drove back to Bellingdale. Obviously her pictures had not given as much pleasure as she had believed. It had been in her mind to try painting some for sale locally, and with the wreaths in winter to augment her meagre income she might have managed. Jugs said the art lecturer had admired them but evidently she had overestimated her own talents even in that direction. She had even finished the picture of springtime to complete the four seasons, intending to give it to Simon as a reminder of new life, a fresh start.

## CHAPTER EIGHT

Roni looked up at the white clouds sailing high in the pale winter sky and made an effort to banish her fears for the future. It was a fine day for the end of February and she determined to get on with her digging. In her heart she knew she could never give up the lodge or her gardens.

She was surprised to hear Dick Ross calling her.

'I have brought you a visitor, Roni.'

'Who?'

Then to her amazement she saw Simon propelling his wheel-chair along the path.

'Dick thought you might be able to find a job for me pricking out seedlings. I must say it's wonderful to be out in the fresh air again.'

He gazed around in appreciation.

'I can understand now why you want to preserve your peace and privacy.'

'Yes.'

Roni smiled, stretching her arms high and wide in the now familiar gesture which captivated Simon.

'I would hate anything to spoil the tranquillity.'

'Your own little piece of heaven. I can't blame you.'

'I could take you up the drive, Simon, if you'd like to look at the rest of the grounds and Bellingdale House,' Dick offered.

'All right,' Simon agreed, and grinned up at Roni. 'Dick has fallen in love with your little mansion. He says he would buy it if he ever won the lottery. But I really did come to work.'

'Enjoy this lovely weather while you can. Jugs has a day off college so he is working on the hen houses. I'll see how he is progressing until you come back.'

She gave them both a smile and a wave and skipped away down the path, her heart suddenly light for no particular reason. Simon watched her with a brooding frown.

'Aye, she moves as gracefully as a ballet dancer,' Dick Ross commented, reading Simon's thoughts, 'but you're coming on well yourself, I hear. Your mother was telling me you can get around quite well with your crutches now that your leg is getting stronger.'

'Yes, I suppose that's always something.'

Simon sighed, but in his heart he knew he ought to cut out the daydreaming. He longed to be able to run after Roni, grab her round the waist and . . . He fought down the bitter regrets with an effort.

Roni and Jugs were discussing the renovations to the wooden hen houses when a large car turned into the drive. A thick-set man emerged and looked around. As Roni scrambled over the planks of wood and jumped on to a narrow path leading to the main drive, she saw a youth getting out of the passenger seat. He looked ill-at-ease and his face was thin and pale. Restless fingers combed through his black hair. He pushed them into his pockets, then pulled them out, twisting his hands together.

'Good morning. Can I help you?' she asked pleasantly.

The man spun round.

'I'm looking for Mr Simon Cole. His mother said we would find him here.'

'He and Mr Ross have gone to see Bellingdale House.'

'I see. Could you take us to him, Miss . . .'

'Kennedy. Yes.'

Roni frowned uncertainly.

'Thank you. Mr Cole may not wish to speak to us, but I'll explain as we go, then perhaps you could ask him before we intrude.'

Roni was dismayed to learn that the man's name was Gordon Campbell and the boy, his only son, was the driver of the car which had knocked Simon down. No wonder he was so ill-at-ease.

'George will have to take his punishment like a man,' Mr Campbell said. 'He understands that, but I want him to see Mr Cole. I want him to realise the damage his foolish escapade has caused to a fellow human being. If Mr Cole will see us, George wants to express his regret in person, face to face. Isn't that right, laddie?'

George mumbled and stared unhappily at the ground. Roni felt uneasy, too, now. How would Simon react? Would he hold her responsible for bringing the Campbells to him? How would he feel, meeting the boy who had ruined his life?

They had almost reached the top of the drive when Roni halted. The front of Bellingdale House had a wide semi-circle of red gravel. Dick Ross and Simon were in the centre of it, gazing up at the house, absorbed in their discussion.

'Maybe you would ask Mr Cole's permission for George to speak to him, Miss Kennedy.'

Mr Campbell seemed uncertain, and almost as agitated as his son now that a meeting with Simon was imminent. Perhaps it was the actual sight of a young, virile man reduced to sitting in a wheel-chair. Roni bit her lip and moved towards the two men. Dick Ross saw her first and smiled in welcome but his smile faded as she explained about the Campbells. Simon jerked his head round to look. The colour drained from his face. Roni fancied she could almost hear his heart racing.

'I'll tell them you don't want to see them if

you'd rather not,' she said.

Simon looked up at her then and took her hand.

'What would you do, Roni?'

'I don't know. Mr Campbell had called at your home first. Don't let them upset you, Simon.'

'Would you like me to talk with them for a minute or two, Simon?' Dick offered. 'It would give you a breathing space to consider.'

'Yes, yes, I'd be grateful, Dick. What did you think of them, Roni?' he added as Dick moved away.

'They're both nervous. The father seems a plain man. He wants his son to realise what he has done. He says they understand that he will have to accept whatever punishment the courts demand. I don't think they are seeking any favours. I believe they are as sorry as it is possible to be. I think they would appreciate it if you would speak to them, if you can, Simon.'

He looked up into her face his colour returning to normal.

'I'm quite sure you're right.'

His grip tightened on her hand.

'Will you stay with me?'

'If that's what you want, of course I'll stay.'

'It is.'

He looked towards the little group.

'Will you bring them over here, Dick?'

The other three moved closer. Simon's fingers clenched so tightly Roni struggled not

to wince. Then George stepped forward. His
eyes looked into Simon's. He shook his head
from side to side, gulped and cleared his
throat but it seemed no words would come.

'I—I am s-sorry, so s-sorry.'

The words were almost a sob.

'I know nothing can make you better again.'

He looked pleadingly at Simon.

'What do you want me to say?' Simon asked
helplessly, but he raised his eyes from the boy
to his father and Mr Campbell stepped
forward.

'There's nothing any of us can say that can
make matters right again,' he said gruffly. 'We
know the law will have to take its course and
George will have to learn his lesson the hard
way. God knows, I'd shield him from that if I
could, but I wanted him to understand what he
has done to you. I don't want him to forget,
ever.'

'I think I understand,' Simon said so calmly
Roni was astonished.

'I want you to know . . .' Mr Campbell
hesitated. 'He's my only son! Can you blame
me for wanting the best lawyer I can get to
defend him, to plead for leniency?'

George trembled and Mr Campbell put a
hand on his shoulder.

'We'll stand by you, son, but you see now
why there is little your mother and I can do.
You do see we can't plead not guilty. We can
only hope for leniency. Your foolishness has

affected Mr Cole for the rest of his life. It's only right that you should face the consequences. Money can't buy your freedom any more than it can put Mr Cole's leg back.'

'I know that, oh, I do, Father. I just wish . . . if only . . .'

'We all wish we could turn the clock back sometimes,' his father said. 'Anyway, Mr Cole, there's just one more thing. I know money can never put things right for you, but I'll see you don't have to wait any longer for compensation. There will be no quibbling over that from us, nor from the insurance company, if I can help it. You've waited long enough as it is, you and your parents. You get your lawyers on to it and I'll see there are no delays. I'd give you everything I have if it could put things right for you, and for my lad, but it can't.'

'No,' Simon said. 'I'm afraid money will not make my leg grow again.'

George winced and Simon looked at him.

'I expect it took a fair bit of courage to come here. I appreciate it.'

They turned and by common consent they began to walk back down the drive.

'We've had a long drive and we hadn't any appetite for food this morning. We'll find a place to have a bite of lunch now. Would you join us, Mr Cole, and your companions, of course?'

'What about it, Simon?' Dick Ross said and Roni guessed he was keen to accept the invitation.

Simon sensed it, too, and wondered what sort of bee Dick had in his bonnet.

'All right,' he agreed reluctantly. 'You'll come, too, Roni?'

'No thanks. I would like to get on with some digging and I have to make some lunch for Jugs.'

'Is he the boy who is hammering?' George asked.

'Yes. He's renovating wooden huts to keep hens, down by the river.'

'Can I see them, Father? Could I stay here until you come back?' George asked with the first sign of animation he had shown since his arrival.

'Stay here? Whatever for, lad?'

'Oh, Father,' the boy said softly, 'I keep telling you and Mother I would rather do things with my hands. I'd like to see what he's making. You know I'm no good at school.'

'Aye, aye, so you keep saying. You're too much like me.' He shrugged. 'We've just made a mess o' things. Oh, go on then and see the lad working, but don't get in his way or hold him back. Is that all right, Miss Kennedy? He's not really a wicked lad.'

'All right.'

Roni nodded. She guessed George was uneasy in Simon's company. It couldn't be easy being confronted by the person you had caused to suffer.

'You can stay, but there's not much here except work.'

The boy nodded.

'I'd like to stay. It's lovely here. I'd like to look around if that's all right.'

Jugs and George Campbell seemed to be getting on amazingly well but Roni wondered what his father would say when he returned to find his son's smart school blazer hung up on a rusty nail, his tie tucked half in and out of a pocket and his shirt sleeves rolled up. The two of them had not heard her approaching to call them for lunch and she could hear them talking companionably as they worked.

She had expected lunch to be a strained affair but Jugs either did not know, or chose to ignore the fact that George Campbell came from a completely different background to either of them. He attended one of the best private schools, and he had never known what it was like to be short of money, but he was certainly not in the least bit arrogant, Roni decided. He appeared to enjoy his food as much as Jugs. In fact in any other circumstances Roni would have considered him a thoroughly nice lad.

It was hard to believe he had taken a car without permission, driven it without a licence, almost killed a man and not even stopped to find out. Except for his nervous fidgeting he seemed almost relaxed in Jugs' company. Roni decided to leave them alone to get on with their repairs.

Much later that afternoon, when the Campbells had driven away and Dick Ross and Simon had left, Jugs told Roni that George Campbell had confided in him about the car accident and how Simon had been injured.

'What'll they do to him, miss?' he asked anxiously. 'He's really, really sorry. He says he can't sleep for thinking about it. He says most days he can't eat either and his mother and his aunt make it worse because they're worried, too.'

'I don't know what will happen, Jugs. It will depend on the courts, I suppose. It is too late to be sorry afterwards, I'm afraid. Nothing can ever make amends to Mr Cole for the loss of his leg.'

'No, I see that. Will they send George to prison?'

'I think they will send him to a young offenders' institution, but I don't know much about these matters.'

'He says his uncle is coming down next week so that his cousin, Dan, can talk to Mr Cole as well. He's going to ask them if he can come back and help me finish the houses for the hens. He wants to be a mechanic like his father but he says his mother wants him to go to university. He says that was partly why he took the car, to prove he could drive it.'

'I see.' Roni sighed. 'I suppose all families have problems of some sort, even when they have lots of money.'

Jugs grinned.

'I wouldn't mind having enough money to buy a car like the Campbells, but I don't think I'd like to be a gentleman if I had to wear a jacket and keep clean all the time.'

The following week-end the weather had changed to blustery winds and sudden showers of sleety rain. Mr Campbell's car pulled into the drive once more, but he had two boys with him this time and they could almost have passed for twins. They had barely climbed out of the car before a smaller car drew in behind them. A man of similar age to Mr Campbell opened the door and literally ejected the driver's seat and himself.

He stood upright, pressed a button and the seat slid back into the car! It was done so smoothly Roni could only stare in amazement. Behind her she heard Jugs gasp.

The two boys moved forward.

'Do you think he'll like it, Uncle Iain?' George Campbell asked anxiously. 'Will it be suitable?'

'We'll make any adaptations he needs if it isn't. We'll go on changing it until it's as perfect for him as we can make it.'

They turned to Roni and Jugs.

'This is Iain Carsewood, my brother-in-law and business partner, and his son, Dan. Iain, this is Miss Kennedy, the enterprising young woman who runs the gardens we were telling you about.'

'Pleased to meet you, Miss Kennedy.'

Iain Carsewood had the same look of strain as his brother-in-law. The two boys had moved close together as though for moral support and George looked almost as terrified as he had the previous week. His cousin clearly shared his trepidation. Jugs seemed oblivious to the air of tension. He moved over to the two boys.

'We'll soon get the huts knocked into shape today, if you've both come to help.'

'My son must speak with Mr Cole before he does anything else,' Iain Carsewood said.

Dan Carsewood bit his lower lip. His face seemed to have turned a shade paler and he twisted his hands together in the same nervous gesture as George. Neither of the boys looked like fifteen-year-olds to Roni. Their misery was so apparent that she almost felt sorry for them, until she remembered how Simon had suffered as a result of their foolish escapade.

'I'm afraid Mr Cole is not here today,' she said.

'Not here?'

Iain Carsewood looked as disappointed as a small boy. He glanced at the car from which he had emerged.

'I make cars for invalids,' he explained. 'It's a sort of hobby of mine. We present them to various charities. I try to adapt them for specific disabilities. It was George's idea that I should adapt one for Mr Cole.'

'I see.'

Roni nodded slowly, wondering if she should send Mr Carsewood to Simon's home.

'I could telephone his home.'

'I expect you think we are trying to wheedle our way into his favour,' Iain Carsewood said, seeing her uncertainty, 'but that's not our purpose. We would give anything for this mess never to have happened, but it has and we all have to suffer the consequences.'

He glanced towards two women, obviously their wives, now standing close together beside a third car. They nodded, clearly wishing themselves anywhere but here.

'This car is a small thing to us, but it could help Mr Cole get back a bit of his independence. I had hoped he might try it out. Gordon thought the drive up to the big house would be a good place to practise.'

'Then I will telephone his home,' Roni said.

It was up to Simon then whether he endured another confrontation or not.

An hour later, Simon and Iain Carsewood were shunting up and down the drive in the car like two schoolboys with a new toy. Dick Ross watched with satisfaction. He knew nothing could make Simon completely whole again, but restoring his independence would go a long way to helping him back to a normal life. Moreover, the firm of Campbell and Carsewood had the engineering expertise to offer him the very best.

Dick had directed the two women to some of the more picturesque villages in the area and they had agreed to meet their husbands for lunch at the Silver Plume. Meanwhile, beside the river, three lads, all clad in bright green boiler suits emblazoned with the Campbell and Carsewood logo, worked in harmony, hammering and sawing to knock the hen houses into shape. Jugs had been delighted when George had tossed him a couple of the firm's protective suits, even if they were rather on the large side!

## CHAPTER NINE

Simon made the most of his new mobility and Iain Carsewood was at pains to make every possible improvement for his convenience and comfort, even to making the rear door open in the opposite direction so that a specially-made wheel-chair could be ejected on to the pavement at the touch of a button. Simon was determined to manage without a wheel-chair as soon as he was fitted with an artificial limb but meanwhile he appreciated Carsewood's efforts to restore his independence.

Jugs took a great interest in every detail and was constantly making small suggestions. Iain Carsewood was impressed and eventually promised him an apprenticeship when he completed his course at the college.

Simon had taken to visiting Bellingdale frequently now that he could get there alone and Roni found herself welcoming his company. She felt more confident in her own surroundings and their conversation ranged widely as they worked side by side pricking out the tiny seedlings.

'The big nurseries do all this with a robot now,' Roni told him wistfully. He slipped an arm around her waist and grinned.

'I much prefer you to any robot, Roni. You and your gardens have given me a new life.'

'No,' she said with a shake of her head, 'you've found the courage to make a new life yourself.'

Even as she said it Roni's heart sank.

'I expect you will soon be picking up the threads and meeting your old friends. You'll soon forget about all this.'

'I couldn't have done it without you, but I still haven't achieved everything I would like.'

'Oh, you'll be doing whatever takes your fancy when you are fitted with your leg. Your mother told me Mrs Black is really pleased with your progress. She says you have more strength in your arms than a blacksmith.'

'There's more to life than learning to walk again. I know that now.'

Two weeks later, Roni was surprised to see Jugs bringing two strangers into the greenhouse where she was working.

'This is Mr McGuire,' he announced importantly. 'He's the head of the art department at the college.'

'Pleased to meet you, Miss Kennedy, and this is a friend of mine, Seamus O'Leary.'

He drew forward a tall, bearded man.

'Seamus has a small art gallery in London and he supplies clients in Britain and America. He happened to drop in at the college just before the Christmas vacation and he saw your water-colour paintings.'

'I did indeed and I can see now where you get such inspiration. I imagine all this will be even more beautiful in a few weeks' time.'

He gestured towards the trees and grounds of Bellingdale.

'I found your pictures delightful.'

'So delightful that he persuaded me to take him to the Coles' after Hogmanay. He tried to buy the paintings from them but they wouldn't sell.'

'Not at any price, young Mr Cole told us,' Seamus O'Leary declared. 'I had great difficulty persuading him to let me borrow them for a few weeks. He agreed eventually when I persuaded him your future could depend upon those pictures. Even then I had to give him my address and credentials and an IOU witnessed by Jeremy.'

'I don't understand.'

Roni stared at him, but her heart was singing. Her paintings had not been relegated to a drawer with old Christmas cards after all.

'I don't know whom you had for a tutor but you certainly have talent, Miss Kennedy, and your love and understanding of your subject shows in your work. Not only that . . .'

He looked at Jeremy McGuire and held out his hands, palms up in a theatrical gesture.

'He's overwhelmed, Miss Kennedy,' McGuire chuckled. 'And that's quite an achievement, I can tell you. Joseph Cole told me you had never been to art college as far as he knew. Is that right?'

'Yes.'

Roni was bewildered.

'Well, if the Coles had possessed a picture of springtime to make up a set of the four seasons, I would have offered them two thousand pounds.'

'Two thousand pounds!'

Roni didn't think she had heard aright. She didn't tell them she had the painting of springtime in the cupboard, or that she had at least twenty small water colours of the garden in all its moods.

'Are you telling me the truth?'

'I am indeed. I've come to offer you a commission. I have one particular client in America who moved over there as a young bride. She said your pictures made her feel quite homesick. She has asked me to get her at least one, but she would be willing to pay really well for a set of four, similar to those you painted for the Coles.'

'I can't believe it!' Roni gasped.

The two men smiled at her. She looked young and innocent and Seamus O'Leary knew he could have made half a fortune out of her work, buying cheaply and selling at its true value. He grimaced to himself. He hadn't the heart to cheat her, and he doubted if young Mr Cole would let him get away with it anyway.

'Really, Miss Kennedy, you ought to get yourself an agent to safeguard your interests. My business is in selling original work, but there are some who make prints and call them limited editions and rip off the artist.'

He pulled out a printed card.

'I'd be greatly obliged if you would contact me at this address and give me an opportunity to offer for your work. I'll come up to Scotland whenever you let me know you have pictures to show me.'

'I don't know what to say,' Roni stammered, but she knew now she would give the picture of springtime to Simon and no-one else.

'But you will think about my offer?' Seamus O'Leary persisted.

'Yes, oh, yes. Thank you.'

'And these are the pictures belonging to your friends.'

He handed her a carefully-wrapped parcel.

'Perhaps you would see they get them safely. We called at the house on the way here but there was no-one at home, and I need to catch the next train back to London. Tell Mr Cole I trust him to send back my IOU.'

Roni was still stunned two hours later when Simon arrived. Jugs had returned to college and she was putting away the lunchtime dishes when he came swinging into her tiny kitchen on his crutches.

'I've had the best news yet, Roni,' he announced jubilantly. 'Can I go through to the living-room?'

'Of course,' Roni replied and followed him.

'We've just come from a meeting with the lawyers. I think I may have the courage to try for my last goal now.'

'Your artificial leg, you mean? I'm sure you'll manage fine.'

'Oh, that. Yes, I'm sure I shall. Roni?'

He hesitated, frowning up at her from the old settee.

'I want your honest opinion. Would an artificial limb stop a girl from wanting to marry a man, do you think?'

Roni's heart plummeted. Had he met someone new, or had one of his old friends come back into his life?

'Roni?' Simon prompted uneasily.

'An artificial limb would be a trivial thing if a girl loved you,' she said sharply and turned away in case he saw the misery she felt.

'Could you learn to love me?' he asked tensely.

She turned back to him, her eyes scanning his face.

'Could you, Roni? Tell me the truth. Could you love someone, knowing he will be a cripple for the rest of his life?'

'You, or just someone?'

'Me.'

'I do love you, Simon,' she said in a voice barely more than a whisper. 'Too much.'

'You could never love me too much!' he said triumphantly. 'Never, never too much. Please do come closer.'

He patted the settee and it was some little while before a flushed and dishevelled Roni regained her senses. It was Simon's talk of weddings, marriage, commitment binding them together for ever, which brought her back to reality.

'I am determined to walk down the aisle so we shall have to wait a while before we set the date for our wedding.'

'We can't . . . I can't marry you, Simon. You must see that.'

'What do you mean?' Simon demanded harshly. 'Are you just pretending? You're not kissing a little boy with a grazed knee. Don't humour me, for pity's sake! We're talking about the rest of our lives! What a fool I've been even to believe you could . . .'

'No, Simon, you are not the one who is foolish. I do love you, but I can never marry you. You are so . . .'

She jerked herself from his arms.

'You would always be ashamed of me in company, especially with your fellow teachers. I couldn't bear it.'

She stared at him, her eyes wide with distress.

'Hey, Roni! I don't understand. What are talking about? You have a chip on your shoulder about teachers.'

'You know the stupid mistakes I make. I couldn't even do my own accounts.'

'But that doesn't matter now. We can work together, help each other, be partners in business, partners in life, and for life.'

'You don't understand,' Roni insisted. 'I tried so hard at school.'

Slowly she began to tell him of the trials which had dogged her schooldays. He listened, beginning to understand why she had such an inferiority complex, even though she was so capable and intelligent, and so lovable. He drew her close, gently this time, smoothing the tendrils of hair from her flushed cheeks.

'I love you more with every passing minute, Roni, but it makes me angry that you have had to suffer so much anguish. Didn't any of your teachers mention dyslexia?'

'Only one, and I was almost ready to leave school then. The rest of them assumed I was either stupid or lazy and sometimes I lost my temper.'

He hugged her, chuckling softly.

'Yes, I can imagine. I expect you'll do the same with me, but think of the fun we shall have making up again. Don't look so stricken, my darling girl.'

He hugged her tightly.

'Lots of people are dyslexic. Some are quite famous, like politicians, actors and racing drivers. I'm no expert but I've had plenty of time on my hands to find out about it. I knew the night I bawled you out how much I had hurt you, how sensitive you are about it. I can't tell you how sorry I was for being such a bear. I love you, just the way you are, but if you really want me to help you, I will. There are even computer programmes to assist us now.'

Roni turned to look at him then, her eyes shining.

'I had a surprise visitor this morning.'

She then told him about Seamus O'Leary's offer for her paintings.

'He hasn't returned the ones he borrowed,' Simon said sharply.

'Yes, he has. He left them with me. And he trusts you to return his IOU. Oh, Simon, I thought you had stuffed the pictures away in a drawer when they disappeared.'

'In a drawer? No way! Mother wanted to tell you, but I thought it would be cruel to raise your hopes if O'Leary was not genuine. It seems I did him an injustice. I'm very glad he appreciates what a talented, young woman you are, my love. I think I may turn out to be a

124

jealous husband though. You are going to marry me, aren't you, Roni?' he asked anxiously.

'If you're sure it is what you want.'

'I'm absolutely sure. Did I tell you I have been awarded preliminary compensation of five hundred thousand pounds in an out-of-court settlement? The rest has to be decided by the lawyers and the insurance company.'

'Five hundred thousand pounds!'

Roni stared up at him.

'Yes. I could never have asked you to be my wife without it. I am too proud, or too old-fashioned, I need to be financially independent, even if I can't be completely independent in other ways. I want to be able to support my wife, and hopefully a family, some day, two things I despaired of ever having a few months ago.'

'Oh, Simon, I . . .'

'I'll do anything in my power to make you happy,' he whispered.

For a while they were both too preoccupied to talk. All Roni's inhibitions were cast aside as she held him tightly, returning kiss for kiss. They didn't hear Dick Ross arriving until he cleared his throat. He chuckled as they sprang apart.

'I called in at Glendocken and your parents told me the good news, Simon. I can't think of a better way to celebrate.'

He grinned widely.

'We have more than that to celebrate,' Simon said proudly. 'Roni has agreed to marry me.'

'Well! I would never have guessed,' Dick teased.

'Will you be best man at our wedding then?'

'I'd be honoured. I've had some news myself.'

'There must be something in the air!' Simon chuckled. 'Tell us, Dick.'

'The Campbells and the Carsewoods are looking into the possibility of buying Bellingdale House. Mrs Campbell is already searching out sponsors.'

He turned to Roni.

'You have made such a good job of saving young Jugs from a life of crime that it gave me an idea. I thought it would be marvellous if something similar could be done for more boys like him and the ones Simon had at his club in Glasgow.'

'I didn't save Jugs,' Roni protested. 'He has done it himself.'

'Only because you gave him the opportunity, and the encouragement, to do something worthwhile. You have done a really good job there, and Jugs is the first to admit it.'

'But not all boys like Jugs would want to garden, or be willing to work as hard as he does,' Roni reminded him.

'No, you're right there, but the aim would

be to have a variety of projects and challenges and not be dependent on charity any longer than we can help. Gordon Campbell and Iain Carsewell have seen for themselves what boredom and frustration can do, even to wealthy kids like their own sons. They are willing to help at week-ends, teaching mechanics, maintaining garden equipment and such like. I can do a bit of building and plumbing myself. Served my time as a builder you know, before I joined the police force. As for Simon here, he could do a lot to help laddies with their studies. Of course, we couldn't manage without you, Roni, to supervise the gardens and organise the kitchens.'

He cast a smiling glance at Simon.

'I think you will have a lot of demands on your time.'

'There is no doubt about that.'

Simon grinned, pulling Roni close again.

'I have already warned her what a demanding husband I mean to be.'

Both men chuckled at Roni's blushes.

We hope you have enjoyed this Large Print book. Other Chivers Press or Thorndike Press Large Print books are available at your library or directly from the publishers.

For more information about current and forthcoming titles, please call or write, without obligation, to:

Chivers Large Print
published by BBC Audiobooks Ltd
St James House, The Square
Lower Bristol Road
Bath  BA2 3BH
UK
email: bbcaudiobooks@bbc.co.uk
www.bbcaudiobooks.co.uk

OR

Thorndike Press
295 Kennedy Memorial Drive
Waterville
Maine 04901
USA
www.gale.com/thorndike
www.gale.com/wheeler

All our Large Print titles are designed for easy reading, and all our books are made to last.